JANET MOORE, *Physical Therapist*

JANET · MOORE,
Physical Therapist

ALICE ROSS COLVER

DODD, MEAD & COMPANY

NEW YORK

Printed in the United States of America
by The Cornwall Press, Inc., Cornwall, N. Y.

For Carol Moon Kaczka, who first gave me the idea
for this book and who helped with its creation

Acknowledgments

I would like to express my thanks to all those who have helped me with the writing of this book. I wish especially to thank Miss Mary Callahan, Director of Courses in Physical Therapy at Columbia College of Physicians and Surgeons, New York City, who was most cooperative in every way and who gave me the introductions I needed; to Miss Althea M. Jones, instructor in the Physical Therapy Department at Columbia College at Physicians and Surgeons, who showed me the entire set-up for Physical Therapy at the Medical Center; to Mr. Aleks Tandyrak, Chief Physical Therapist of the Veterans Administration Hospital in New York City who took me on a personally conducted tour there; to Miss Blanche Talmud, Supervising Therapist at the Institute for Crippled and Disabled in New York City, who was so generous with her time and her interest when I visited her; to Janet Gail Beeler whose enthusiasm for her work was infectious and who kindly gave me considerable assistance during her last busy weeks as a student of Physical Therapy at Columbia College of Physicians and Surgeons; and, finally, to Winifred Moon and Carol Moon Kaczka, Graduate Physical Therapists, both of whom helped me greatly by checking my facts and answering my many questions.

ALICE ROSS COLVER

Contents

Contents

JANET MOORE, *Physical Therapist*

1

The Quarrel

IT ALL STARTED WITH A QUARREL.

There she was, practically engaged to Dick Forsythe, even though she had no ring, and they had to go and quarrel! And over what? Over nothing that should be quarreled about, Janet thought. But he had thought differently and she couldn't change his mind and he couldn't change hers and their words had grown sharper and sharper until, suddenly, each of them had become stiff and cold and remote—like strangers. And finally she had said slowly, "Well, I guess we'll have to agree to disagree."

And he said, equally slowly, "I guess we will—if that's the way you want it." He had added, "I'm sorry." And then he had waited . . . as if he thought she might say the same thing and it would be the beginning of making up. But she had been too hurt and surprised and—and bewildered by it all, so she had said nothing. Nothing at all. And then he got up and moved away out of the moonlight and the roses that had made the world so beautiful that night. Out of all that. And out of her life. Forever, she thought.

That had happened only two and a half days ago. And now here she was, walking along the curved sidewalk past Rhododendron Hollow toward the little stone chapel, her black graduation gown swinging rhythmically, the tassel on her mortared cap dangling, and her heels seeming to hammer out only one thing over and over again: *All through college and no place to go. All through college and no place to go.*

Did she mean she wished she really were going to marry Dick right away and settle down into being a housewife and nothing else? Janet asked herself. No! A thousand times *no!* What she meant was she hadn't chosen yet what career she would take up. That's all she meant.

No regrets for Dick Forsythe! There were other men in the world. Men with broader ideas than he had. Men less selfish. Men who would be proud of her ambitions and desires. Maybe she had shocked him a little but that wasn't any excuse for him to be so old-fashioned, so—so—obtuse. And stubborn. Just because he was four years older than she was didn't make him that much wiser, necessarily, so that he was right on this thing. But he wasn't. She was sure of that.

Her roommate, Ann Wickers, marching beside her, spoke in a low voice.

"Janet Moore! What's the matter with you? You're going much too fast! You can hear the organ from the chapel now, so slow down! Keep in step!"

Janet slowed. But she was thinking tumultuously, "I want to get there! I want to have my diploma handed to me and pack out of here and *begin.*"

Begin what? Never mind what. Something!

The slow, swinging walk forward continued. The black gowns swayed. The little tassels bobbed. Presently, Janet was mounting the chapel steps and moving down the center aisle toward the first ten or fifteen rows of seats where the Seniors were all grouped together in front of their parents, friends, and other guests. There was singing. There was a prayer. There were speeches. Finally, there was a commencement address by an outside notable. Then their own white-haired college president took the rostrum and, in a few moments, she was reading out slowly the names of all the graduates and Janet was stepping forward to accept her rolled and beribboned sheepskin. And then she was on her way down the aisle again, past all the smiling families and out to the chapel steps where she would wait for her folks . . . and once more her heels were hammering out a little tune.

All through college and no place to go.

Because where was she going? What was she going to do? In spite of all her positive words to Dick, she didn't know. Off and on, she had thought of two or three things in a vague way but she hadn't felt she had to decide at once. She would take a few weeks—maybe the whole summer— to consider this and that. She would talk it all over with Dick, too, first, of course. Well, now she had talked it over with him—

Against her will, her mind went back to that night of moonlight and roses and Dick and the moment that had brought her to this impasse.

He had come that evening—last Friday, before her parents arrived—because he couldn't get off on Monday, today, to be present at her commencement. His was a new job—computer programming in a big electrical company. At least it was new to him and he couldn't, so near the beginning of it, ask for a free day. She understood that, of course. Actually, to come then, when he had to go back that same night because of something unexpected to do on Saturday, meant eight hours of driving for him—four up and four back. He wouldn't reach Connecticut again—where he lived in a bachelor apartment—until three or four in the morning, the very best he could do. She'd known that, so she hadn't expected him last weekend at all and his telephone call was a complete surprise. He had telephoned to her on his way up and told her not to eat until he got there.

They had gone to the little inn in the college town where, after a very late dinner, they had found the broad veranda surrounding it nearly deserted. Back in a far corner there was a swing, hidden from the street by clambering roses through which the moonlight filtered. How happy she had been, sitting there with him! She could see his face now the way it had been then, dark and serious, as he turned to her and said, "Now let's make plans. Can't we be married this month?"

This month! She had been startled. How long had she known him, anyway? Only since Christmas. And this was just June. She had met him at a dance at the country club during the holidays in her home town of Oakwood. He had been visiting his married sister who lived there, when he had come East from the Midwest for some job interviews in and around New York City, which was not far away. When Molly Evans had brought him over to introduce him, something about him had made her heart stop. He said, much later, it had been the same with him. Anyway, he had made his home with Molly for three or four months, until he had located his present position with the electric company in Connecticut, and during all that time they had seen each other almost every weekend, after she returned to college, drifting, without too many words, into a happy but indefinite relationship that seemed to take the future for granted. But it had simply never occurred to her that he would want to get married so soon.

Shocked, she had said as much, and he had answered, "Well, why not? You're through college and so am I. I also have my Ph.D., and a job—a good job with a good future. So why not? What's there to wait for?"

"Well, I—I—" She had found herself stuttering helplessly but he had knocked all clear thinking out of her head for a moment. Quickly, she groped for words. "I want to *prove* myself before I get married, Dick. I want to do something and prove that I can. I don't want all these four years of study to be—to be wasted."

"You mean you want a career?" he asked incredulously. "I never dreamed—"

"Yes! That's it. I want a career," she interrupted.

"But marriage is a career," he had said gently. And the caressing quality in his voice went through her, as it always did, so that she had to armor herself against it and against weak acquiescence to him. They had had spirited discussions before but never heated ones. This time, however, she had been frightened by his sudden demand. It was as if her freedom were threatened—the freedom to which she had been looking forward after four years of college—as if her independence were lost before she had fully acquired it. It made her answer with sudden anger.

"Oh! It is *not* a career! That's an obsolete point of view! What do I do as a bride? I cook and clean. That's all. Anybody can cook if she can read these days. It's simple. And any moron can clean. What kind of career is that for an educated person?"

He had looked at her in astonishment and his tone was firm and no longer caressing when he replied. "It's enough for some women, Janet. It's enough for my sister Molly."

"She has two children! That's different. Anyway, it wouldn't be enough for me—not at first. It's no challenge. What does it offer in all the free time I'd have? Bridge parties." She spoke the word with contempt. "That's all. It's not enough, Dick."

He was thoughtful for a moment, still looking at her as if she were some one new and different that he'd never seen before. Then he said, "I see. Well, get a job, if you like. I've no objection—as long as it doesn't interfere with our married life."

"As long as I'm there to get your breakfast before you leave and there with dinner ready when you get home, you mean!"

"Yes," coolly, "that's exactly what I mean. What's wrong with that?"

"It's colossally selfish!" she had cried hotly. "That's what's wrong with it! You don't want me to develop myself! You just want me to take any piddling little job—like selling bobby pins in the Five-and-Ten—as long as I'm there to cook for you when you want to eat!"

He had laughed a little at that point. Laughed! When she was so serious.

"Oh, come on, Janet!" he had demurred. "I didn't say that."

"You didn't have to say it. You meant it, though."

"Well, for the matter of that, what else can you do other than some piddling job?" he had asked. "Listen! Let's be reasonable. You're not trained for anything. You'd have to go to a secretarial school or some kind of school if you wanted a really decent job—a career. And that would take another year."

"So what if it did take another year?" she had flashed. "What's a year? We've got a whole lifetime ahead of us!"

There was an instant of silence. Then—"I don't want to wait a year," he had said quietly. "I'm twenty-six. And I've found you. And I'm satisfied. I don't want to wait."

"Well, I *do*."

"You mean"—he spoke very slowly—"you're not satisfied with me? You're not sure you'd like to marry me?"

"When you talk like this—no! I'm *not* sure!" She had wanted to catch back the words but they were said. And although she had tried, she had not been able to make him believe that that was not really what she meant. She meant she wanted a year in which to find herself—to try her wings —to show her parents that all the money they had spent on her for college hadn't been thrown away, that she had a contribution to make to the world because of it, that—

Oh! She couldn't remember all that had been said! She only remembered that she had suddenly discovered that they didn't see things alike at all. It was a jolt. The crux of the matter was so simple. She wanted to wait a year and he didn't. That was the whole of it. But the more she tried to explain herself, the further away he seemed to go from her. She ended by saying she thought he was selfish and reactionary and bigoted, and he said he didn't just think— he *knew*—she was young and impulsive and not yet sure of her own mind. She not only didn't know what she wanted to do with the year she was talking about, she also didn't know whether or not she loved him.

"And that," he had told her with grave reluctance, "settles the matter as far as I'm concerned. I don't want you if you're not certain about me. It's too big a risk."

"We agree to disagree, then," she had answered, and the words fell cold and hard between them and lay there like ice pellets. He had nodded . . . and then he had stood up and the moonlight fell whitely on his face, but it did not touch his eyes, so she could not see what they held, whether relief or grief.

"I'm sorry," he had said, after a queer, stifled moment, not sounding really sorry at all, only grim and—and final. "But if this is the way you want it—okay."

The way *she* wanted it! When it was *he*, not she! But before she could expostulate about that, he was gone. He was gone and she was free—free to take her year and do whatever she wished to do.

But what, exactly, was that?

—*through college and no place to go,* her heels said as she walked down the chapel steps, her diploma in her hand.

Well, she would find a place. Right away. Why, there were a million places to go! Surely she could find one.

The president's reception to all the graduates and their

guests was to be held on the lawn of the president's home, down by the lake. After her parents met her under the trees outside the chapel, Janet arranged for them to wait for her in the lounge of her own dormitory, then they would all three walk to the reception together. But first, she told them, she would hurry ahead to her room, in order to shed her cap and gown, which was dreadfully hot, and to finish her last bit of packing.

Arriving there, she found the place empty. She tossed her tasseled mortarboard onto her stripped bed and the gown after it. These had been rented and Ann, who was not to leave until tomorrow, had said she would return them for her roommate, together with her own. Then Janet walked to her dismantled bureau to freshen her make-up and tidy her hair. The mirror gave back an oval face coming down to a determined chin, wide-spaced, candid, hazel eyes above a nose that held a light sprinkling of tiny freckles, and above the nose thick, short bright hair which held a natural wave.

Powdering her nose, Janet leaned closer to peer at herself. Did anything show of what she was feeling? She had thought her father gave her a rather sharp glance back there by the chapel. Not that she had any feelings left about Dick. That was over. Incredible but true. It was the other thing. The uncertainty ahead. The sudden realization that she was really at an end and that a new beginning was in order for her. She had thought—when Dick was in her life—that there would just be a going on, a continuing in familiar ways and a familiar pattern, even without college. But now she knew that that was not so. Now she couldn't bear the thought of idling through a whole summer with nothing definite planned, for life would be too different with Dick out of the picture. Everything would be different. Everything!

She touched her lipstick to her mouth, ran a comb through her tawny hair, and adjusted the shoulder of her white commencement dress. It was V-necked, with tiny short sleeves and a fluttering pleated skirt. Pearls were her only adornment until she turned to a glass on the window sill that held a white orchid. Lifting it out, she pinned it at the V of her dress. Dick had had the decency to send that, anyway—unless it had been ordered before he had a chance to cancel it.

Suddenly, the numbness that had held her in its grip ever since Friday night left her and she felt like weeping. To her horror, a sound like a sob escaped her. Angrily, she shook her head, dabbed at the tears that had rushed to her eyes, powdered her nose again, picked up her small white handbag, and quickly left the room. No hysterics, Janet, she told herself. A man who wants just a—a slave for a wife is no loss to any girl.

Downstairs, Mr. and Mrs. Moore were waiting for Janet and it was with relief that she joined them, glad to escape from herself. Glad, too, to be with them. She must be peculiar, she thought fleetingly, because she seemed to be practically the only girl in her class who got along so beautifully with her family. She adored her tall father with his gray hair and scholarly face and absolutely perfect manners. She loved his calmness and his dispassionate view of everything and the quiet, humorous way he managed her more volatile mother. It was Mrs. Moore's quick impetuosity that made her seem so young and that gave her a special sparkling charm. And how pretty she was, Janet's thoughts went on, with hair that was still golden—except around the edges—and her small-featured, eager face. Coming up to them both now, Janet felt a surge of pride to have parents that looked and acted as hers did, and she was glad she didn't have to share them with any brothers or sisters.

The three of them were joined at the last minute by Ann Wickers and her family. They all walked to the president's reception together, so it was not until much later that Janet had a chance to speak of the matter so close to her heart. By that time, she had packed up the last of her possessions, had changed into a lightweight suit, had said all her good-bys, and she and her mother and father had betaken themselves in their loaded car to the inn for dinner. (The same inn where she and Dick had been a few evenings ago!) Afterward, they would make the rather long drive back to their home in Oakwood.

Their order for the meal given, Janet leaned forward, put both elbows on the table, and spoke with her usual forthrightness.

"Mother. Dad. I want to tell you something. Dick and I have broken off and I don't want to say anything more than that except we're really through. I didn't know him as well as I thought I did and I found out Friday night that he's not at all what I believed he was. He's—he's reactionary and narrow-minded and stubborn and selfish, and we're *through*. So now I have to think about another kind of future and I may need your help—if you can bear to give it to me a while longer." She stopped, breathless, her wide eyes not quite hiding the turmoil in her heart.

This her father saw, but he regarded her with a calm, untroubled gaze. Her mother, however, gave a small, shocked gasp, so that her father spoke quickly. "Now, Jeanette! There's nothing to get excited about. A woman always has the privilege of changing her mind, you know. As for helping you, Janet, you may be sure it's our pleasure as long as you need it. What had you thought of as an alternative to matrimony?"

"That's it. I hadn't got that far. I only know I want to do something. I don't much care what so long as it's useful and important. But Dick doesn't want me to do anything. He just wants me to be a parasite. And that's why we've parted company."

"I see."

How steady he was. How reassuring, somehow. Janet was grateful to him—to them both—for not asking any questions or trying to argue with her about Dick, whom she knew they both liked very much. He went on carefully. "Let's think now. What could you do? Something lucrative, I suppose you have in mind?"

"Well, preferably, of course. But—" Unbidden, Dick's words came back to her mind. *"You're not trained for anything. You'd have to go to a secretarial school or some kind of school if you wanted a really decent job—a career."*

Was he right? She went on a trifle uncertainly, "I suppose I could be a receptionist in a doctor's office—"

"Darling!" Her mother's vehement protest interrupted her. "Any high-school graduate can get a job like that. Don't cheapen yourself. You've a college degree."

"I know, but I've had no training for anything, Mother.

I doubt if I could get into an office anywhere without taking stenography or typing first."

Her father spoke. "Perhaps things aren't as bad as all
that. There are some untrained college girls who are finding positions every year, although I admit stenography and
typewriting help. Do you want to go to a secretarial school,
Janet?"

Quite suddenly and definitely Janet knew she didn't.
She couldn't see herself in any kind of office, doing secretarial work, and she said so. "It just doesn't appeal to me
at all. I'm sort of—at sea," she admitted, "because I don't
want to teach, either."

"What about the Peace Corps? Have you thought of
that?"

"Dad! Janet's voice and face held dismay. "Do you want
to get rid of me? Is that what you're saying?"

"Darling!" Again her mother's quick remonstrance,
joined this time by her father's deep-toned and positive,
"*No*. Of course not. I just wondered if you'd thought of it.
That's all."

"Yes, I've thought of it, but, frankly, I've no special yen
to go to some far-off land. In the first place, I like it at
home—being with you both, I mean."

"That's very flattering." Mr. Moore smiled affectionately
at his daughter. "And we certainly like having you stay at
home. After all, you've been away from us for four years.
And in time you'll marry, if not Dick, someone else, then
you'll be gone for good. So if you have no yen, as you say—"

"I haven't. I'm sure of that. And I'm sure about the
secretarial school, too. I just can't see myself at a type-

writer all day. Besides, getting back to the Peace Corps, it's my private opinion that this country has done about enough in foreign aid. Why not help some of the people in America who need help? There must be plenty of them."

"There are." Mrs. Moore spoke quickly. "You only have to work in a hospital, as I do, to find that out. By the way, Janet, *that* is something that's open to you and that doesn't require stenography or typing—just a willing heart and two hands. It's not lucrative, of course—you'd be a volunteer—but until you find out exactly what it is you want—" she stopped, not wishing to urge too much but hopeful, for being head of the volunteer groups in the hospital at Oakwood was her greatest interest.

"Well"— Janet looked at her mother with considering eyes—"I wouldn't mind—for a while—to fill up time until, as you say, I know—"

How little did she realize that her hesitant words were signing and sealing the direction of her future!

2

❀

A Goal Is Found

J ANET CAME UP OUT OF THE SUBWAY in New York near the
entrance to the Presbyterian Medical Center, glanced
around for a moment to get her bearings, then walked
quickly to the corner of Broadway and West 168th Street.
Here she turned left toward the Hudson River. She was
looking for number 630, which, she discovered, was on the
left side of the street, more than halfway down the block.

As she went up the steps and through the wide entrance
doors her heart quickened its beat, for she was about to
enter a new world, a new life. This was the beginning of
that year she had decided to take—at least, she hoped it
would turn out that way. It all depended on the interview
ahead of her.

Pausing by the information desk, just inside at her right,
she addressed the attendant there.

"I'm looking for the Physical Therapy department. Miss
Mallory's office."

"Third floor, miss. Room 431. Take the elevator at the
rear."

Janet spoke her thanks and moved down the hall to where an elevator stood open. A tall, well-built young man in a blue sports shirt, carrying his coat slung over his arm, strode by her as she reached it, then stood aside as he saw she was about to enter the car, too. Nodding to him, she stepped in and said to the operator, "Third, please."

"Same here," said the young man, and looked directly at her. "P.T.?" he asked.

"What?" She glanced up into a pair of probing, bright blue eyes set in a square, very tanned face beneath a thatch of unruly blond hair bleached almost white by the sun. "Oh! Physical Therapy, you mean. Yes, that's where I'm going." She hesitated. "Are you?" He might be an instructor, she thought, although he seemed young for that.

"Yes, I've been accepted—finally. Now I have to pick up my approved program and then go pay my fees at the bursar's office. I'm a little late doing this. I guess you are, too."

"I didn't know men took this course," Janet said in surprise, ignoring his question.

"Why not?" And his sudden grin, flashing whitely from the bronze of his face, was most attractive.

Why not, indeed? she asked herself as the elevator stopped and they both stepped out.

"This way," he told her as she hesitated, and she moved along with him toward a door on the left where a small sign indicated it was the Physical Therapy department. Again he stood aside to let her enter.

"Name's Plunkett," he said, out of the corner of his mouth as she passed him. "David Plunkett. And I'll be seeing you."

A small, middle-aged woman rose from a desk across the room and came forward.

"Mr. Plunkett? Oh, yes. Your forms are here and approved. That's all you want, isn't it? You're welcome. We're glad you're going to be with us. And you?" She looked inquiringly at Janet as David vanished through the door. "Miss Moore? I remember now. You telephoned a few days ago. You have an appointment with Miss Mallory. Come right this way." And she led Janet toward a door to an inner office. "Miss Mallory? Miss Moore is here to see you."

A woman in her early thirties rose from her desk as Janet stepped into the room and held out her hand in greeting. She had short, graying hair, gray eyes, and a warm, friendly voice.

"I'm so glad to meet you, Miss Moore. Sit down, won't you? We have a good many things to talk over, I believe. Now, then, where shall we begin? Suppose you tell me first why you think you want to take up the study of Physical Therapy?"

Janet settled into the chair facing Miss Mallory. How could she ever get into a few brief words her discovery that this was exactly what she wanted to do? It was not an impulsive decision. She had found out through trial and error that it was the thing she had been looking for so earnestly. She was as certain of it as she was of sitting here this hot July morning, having this interview.

After the graduation exercises were all over, there had been the long drive from college to Oakwood, during which Janet had fallen asleep in the back seat. Then her arrival with her parents, about midnight, at the big, sprawling white house set on a half acre of land that was the Moore home. She had not unpacked that night, although her father had helped her carry up to her room most of her things from the car. (Her trunk would come along later by express.) She had, instead, dropped into her own bed and there she had stayed through half of the next day.

When she woke, the house was quiet. She lay still for a long moment, her eyes roving about the familiar setting. She loved it. She loved the dainty white furniture, the deep blue rug on the floor, the tiny flowered pattern of the wallpaper, the crisp, snowy curtains at the windows—everything. She was glad to be through with dormitory life. She was glad to be home. Only—

Only what was she going to do with herself all the time? Dick's going out of her life had really left a big hole. But she wouldn't think about him. There were a couple of weddings coming up at which she was to be a bridesmaid. These meant several days away, maybe a week altogether. When they were over and she really settled down here, there would be tennis to keep her busy. She could enter the tournament matches. There was also swimming at the club pool. And dances every Saturday night in the great clubroom. But—oh, dear!—everyone would ask her about Dick and she would have to tell them something—she didn't know quite what—although she shrank from the thought.

Dick again! She couldn't help but think about him, for now, in the stillness of the morning, she realized sharply just what his withdrawal meant. No nightly telephone calls from Connecticut. No planning for the weekends. No sudden surprise visits. No unexpected letters. With a little ache in her heart, she began remembering about him. The way he had looked the first time she had seen him when Molly had brought him over to introduce him at the club. His tall, straight figure and the proud way he held his shoulders when he walked. The slight cleft in his squared-off chin. The b᾿᾿ ᴏf a wave in his thick, dark hair. His dark eyes, so direct ᾳ ᴅ serious and searching. They had seemed to look right through her and then, suddenly, they had turned into warm twin fires as he smiled at her, and her heart had done a somersault and she had thought at once— *I like him.*

Yes, she had liked him then, and the more she saw of him, the more she liked him. She liked his devotion to his sister Molly. His helpfulness when she had her hands full with the children, who, incidentally, adored him. They rushed to him when he arrived and clung to him while he was there, and with both of them he played games as if he were their same age and loved their activities as much as they did. But Kitty seemed to be his favorite. There appeared, in fact, to be a special secret bond between them. He had also been companionable with Brent, Molly's husband. While toward her own family he had shown the same unfailing courtesy and consideration she had always found in her father.

Was it because he was older than the college boys she knew that she had fallen so hard for him? It had been flattering, of course, because he was three years ahead of them all. The difference made him seem purposeful and equipped for life. Indeed, she wondered if he had ever floundered as, for example, Scott Murray had floundered?

She couldn't imagine it. Dick Forsythe seemed to her always to have been sure of his direction. It gave him a quiet strength and confidence that were impressive. It gave him a masterfulness, too—and she had liked that masterfulness until the time he had carried it too far and had assumed their future together in the pattern *he* had chosen.

Well—he was gone, and she mustn't spend any more time thinking about him.

Janet got out of bed and showered in her own bathroom, then dressed for the day in white shorts and a sleeveless white blouse. When she went downstairs to get some coffee, the cleaning woman told her that her mother had gone out.

"To the hospital, she say. And if you want to go there, too, she say she be looking for you."

Janet nodded and removed a crumb of toast from the shining surface of the mahogany dining table. Should she go? Or shouldn't she? Somehow a great lassitude lay on her and she didn't want to do anything—not anything at all. Now that college and everything were over and nothing much lay ahead, she had neither interest nor ambition. She had told her mother she would help at the hospital— true—but she hadn't said when she would begin and she knew her mother wouldn't push her.

Somehow she got through the day. Somehow she made herself go to the club and face everyone and announce publicly that she and Dick were waging a cold war. Let that do, for the present, she thought. She had said it with a bright laugh and a toss of her tawny head so that no one need think she cared. Then she had plunged into a tennis game and after that she had taken a swim in the pool and after *that* she had gone home for dinner with her parents and a long, lonely evening which she spent playing the records that had been Dick's and her favorites.

That day became a pattern for her—excepting the times when she went to the weddings of her two classmates. Only the evenings varied. The moonlight and the music—alone —that first night were more than Janet could bear, so, after that she seized upon the numerous activities suggested by someone of the crowd—a cookout; a car full of good companions to drive to the movies over at Lake Macabee; a theater expedition to New York. . . . She felt driven to escape from herself. But nothing she did fully satisfied her. It was just a way of passing time. It had no point and no purpose and, besides, it was all too familiar. About the time she acknowledged to herself that she couldn't keep on in such a fashion indefinitely, her mother reminded her of her promise.

"It's the month of July, Janet, and people are taking their vacations, which makes us awfully short-handed at the hospital. You could really be a great help as a volunteer. How about trying it?"

So Janet had tried. She had donned a "pink lady" uniform and had found herself filling in everywhere, doing all kinds of different things. Sometimes she was at the reception desk, sometimes she was pushing the library cart around to the various wards and rooms, sometimes she was writing letters for patients, sometimes she was serving food from behind the high counter in the cafeteria. It was always interesting, whatever she did, and it opened her eyes for the first time to the great need for workers in the sprawling hospital.

By now, summer was fully upon them, with its hot, sticky days. Still Janet, discovering how indispensable she was, did not give up her volunteer work. For one reason, it had opened up a new world to her, so that her thoughts about her future were becoming clearer. She knew now that her experience among the sick interested her greatly. She knew, too, that she enjoyed working with people. And she knew she liked the knowledge that her services were truly helpful. However, she was equally certain that she did not want to spend the rest of her life doing the countless little things she was now doing because anybody, really, could do them. Any high-school graduate. Indeed, anybody at all.

"You might just as well never have sent me to college," she said to her father one night. "I mean, I don't feel properly used! I'm used *up* at the end of a day but I'm not fully *used*, if you follow me."

"Your potentialities aren't used. Yes. But don't feel that college has been wasted," he had replied cheerfully. "You'll find the answer to the thing you're seeking someday."

And then, soon after that, miraculously, Janet had found it.

She had gone into the women's ward to write letters for any patients who might want that service and had just seated herself next to an old lady whose eyes were bandaged when a blue-uniformed aide came in with a wheel chair and stopped at the next bed.

"All ready to go for your treatment, girlie?" she asked brightly.

Janet, turning her head, saw a child of about ten, with

big eyes in a pale face, who could scarcely move her legs, being helped into the wheel chair by the aide. Suddenly, from the wide entrance door at the end of the long room came a low call.

"Miss Flint! Emergency, Miss Flint! Please! Emergency!"

"Oh, my goodness!" The aide had exclaimed and had looked distractedly from the little girl to the nurse calling her at the door. Then her glance lit on Janet. "Will you take Dora? I've got to go, and they're waiting for her in the treatment room. It's her time. Take her to the Physical Therapy department on the third floor, will you? Thanks. Please wait there with her, to bring her back if I don't get there in time. Okay?" And she was gone, her white apron flying as she hurried away.

Janet leaned over the old lady with the bandaged eyes and explained that she would be back later to write the letter for her. Then she smiled down at the child waiting in the wheel chair.

"You'll have to show me the way. I've never been there," she said.

"Oh, I'll show you! I've been there lots of times. They're making me well up there."

"Are they? How wonderful!"

It was, indeed, Janet's first visit to the treatment room and it was a revelation to her. She watched silently as Dora, chatting happily with a girl in a white dress, was lifted by her onto an exercise table where she was put through a series of carefully calculated leg movements.

"How do you know what to do?" Janet asked presently. "How do you know you aren't hurting her? Are you a nurse? You haven't a nurse's uniform or cap on."

"No, I'm not a nurse. I'm a Physical Therapist." The girl nodded over her shoulder toward the emblem sewn onto her left sleeve and Janet saw a triangle outlined in black on a white ground, with the letters PT in black in the middle. "Rita Wilks by name. And I only do what the doctor tells me to do. It's all written down for me on Dora's chart. She's making wonderful progress," she went on. "I expect we'll have her standing up and maybe even walking a bit before the summer's over. Won't we, Dora?"

"I hope so. I *bet* so!" Dora amended, her dark eyes lighting up.

"I bet so, too. Look around if you like," Rita added to Janet. "You might care to see what goes on here while I'm working with Dorrie."

So Janet gazed around. She saw strange-looking machines, oddly shaped tubs of water, wall pulleys with weights attached, and a contraption that seemed to be all slings and springs. She saw more familiar apparatus, too, such as she herself had used in the gymnasium at college— parallel bars and floor mattresses and wall bars. She saw crippled people using these things under the watchful eyes of the two other Physical Therapists in the room, and all of them seemed cheerful. A little Negro boy with one leg dangling much shorter than the other was being taught how to walk on his good leg, using low parallel bars as crutches. A man sat on a table, regularly lifting in the air one foot to which a heavy weight was attached. An elderly woman was working away at a pulley that helped her raise her arms above her head. She smiled at Janet.

"See!" she said. "When I began this exercise I couldn't get up any higher than my shoulders. And now look!"

Janet smiled back at her. "Good for you!" she answered.

She looked around a while longer and saw a young girl with a leg amputated below the knee enter the room and discard her crutches as she was helped to attach an artificial leg and then to walk on it. Janet also saw a boy wheeled in who was assisted onto a stationary bicycle, which he pedaled with difficulty but with great determination. Everywhere she looked there were people learning to live with their handicaps, or, rather learning to live in spite of them. Thoughtfully, she went back to the exercise table and spoke to Rita, who was in charge of little Dora.

"I'd like to ask you some questions whenever you have the time," she said.

"Certainly. Right now. What do you want to know?"

Janet could not quite understand why she was so intrigued by this room, but it seemed to tell her clearly that this was what she would rather be doing in the hospital than all the trivial things she had been doing. It was not only more interesting. It was more inspiring because it was so truly constructive. So she had asked questions and received answers—and they had brought her to New York and Miss Mallory's office today.

"I found out," she said now to Miss Mallory, "that being a 'pink lady' wasn't sufficiently satisfying. I found out, too, that I'd have to take a course in Physical Therapy if I wanted to work in that department in our hospital at home. As ours doesn't offer training along that line and this was the nearest place for me to get it—Rita Wilks recommended it to me. She graduated from here. I came in today to see you and find out what the requirements are."

Miss Mallory looked at Janet and liked what she saw—
a frank, sensitive face, with clear, steady eyes and a determined chin. A face that was friendly and eyes that were
unafraid.

She said, "Yes, I remember Rita. Well, we require for
entrance into the Physical Therapy course here either two
years of college or a college degree. You can come in as a
college Junior and take two years to finish or you can come
in as a graduate and finish in one year."

"I have a degree," Janet told her. "I graduated last
month from Williston College, with a Liberal Arts degree."

"Fine! That's a good place. But you know registration
here takes place in June for the next September class.
You're late."

"I'm sorry about that, but I couldn't help it. I didn't
know until a few days ago that this was what I wanted to
do. Am I too late?"

"Perhaps not. We'll see. First, I have to have a transcript
of all the courses you took at Williston. Have you, for
example, had sociology? And biology?" When Janet gave
a double affirmative answer, Miss Mallory went on. "That's
good. What about physics? And social science? And psychology?"

"I've studied all those, too," Janet said and added, "I
majored in psychology."

Miss Mallory nodded approvingly. "Well, I must know
exactly how many hours you've had in each of those subjects, so suppose you send right away for a complete transcript of all your work covered at Williston. When I get

that, I can then tell if you're eligible for admission to our fall class."

"I'll write to my college today, as soon as I get home." Janet paused. Was the interview over? She spoke impulsively. "If you can give me a little more time, Miss Mallory, I have a lot of questions I'd like to ask."

"Certainly. That's what I'm here for—to answer questions."

"Well, in the first place, at the end of the year—if I complete the course—what would I receive? Do you give degrees in Physical Therapy?"

"No, Miss Moore, we give Bachelor of Science degrees to those who are with us for two years and graduate. But you already have a degree, so you would receive a Certificate of Proficiency in Physical Therapy. You would, however, be considered as well qualified as the degree girls to practice your profession."

"I see. Then next June I'd be all set to take a job?"

"Again no, not next June. You would have eight months, from September through May, to study theoretical and technical subjects, here at Columbia. Your actual clinical practice—which you must have—does not begin until summer. You would have to spend June, July, August, and September doing clinical work in various affiliated hospitals, so that you wouldn't, actually, be ready to take a position until a full year after you enter here."

"I see," said Janet once more. She was silent a moment, her eyes thoughtful. I told Dick a year and that's what it's going to be, she was thinking. Then she went on, "Now about expenses. Is it going to cost the earth? Dad has already paid for four years of college. I hate to ask him to stake me to anything more, although he has been darling about it. He says, if I'm sure this is what I want—" She broke off. "How much will it cost, please? I promised him I'd find out."

Miss Mallory reached into a drawer of her desk, saying, "Here's a booklet you had better take home to your father. In it you'll find all your questions answered. I can tell you now, however, that the tuition is twelve hundred and fifty dollars this year. It goes up a little every year, I'm sorry to say. Then there are other expenses, of course—for books and a hospital fee and subway and bus fares and your late registration fee—" She stopped.

"And my board and room," Janet added.

"Yes, plus your living expenses, of course, whether you live in Johnson Hall, which is the girls' dormitory, or at International House, or rent a furnished apartment with another girl—" She broke off at Janet's exclamation.

"You mean it's possible to live in an apartment?" Her eyes shone. She would love that! She was tired of dormitory living.

"Yes, it's quite possible. We can give you a few recommended addresses but you make your own arrangements with an agent or the owner. In any case, wherever you live, the cost is about the same. You would have to figure on another thousand or so for that expense, making the total—well—in the neighborhood of twenty-five hundred dollars or even a bit more." She looked at Janet consideringly. The expense was so often a stumbling block.

"Of course there are ways of earning money while you're here," she added. "That young man, Mr. Plunkett, who came in with you, plans to work his way through. There are all kinds of jobs open. Typists, waitresses, technicians, for example. And there are loans available, too, from a number of sources. Local patriotic organizations, like the American Legion, or industrial organizations, or state scholarships. Then there's the National Foundation. All of these can help you. Oh, yes! There are federal loans, also. You can contact our main office at 1790 Broadway, if you want to find out more about getting financial aid."

Janet drew a long, slow breath. "I'm lucky," she said frankly. "I don't think I'll have to work my way while I'm here. And I don't think Dad would want me to take a loan from anyone. But it's nice to know these things can be managed. I was surprised," she went on, "to discover that you take men students in Physical Therapy. Are there many?"

"There will be three in the Certificate course this fall. David Plunkett is one. He wants to be a doctor but he can't afford either the time or the money for training, so this is a compromise."

Janet nodded understandingly. The young man's bleached hair could mean he was a lifeguard somewhere, she thought. He certainly had the physique for it.

"How many of us would there be altogether? Graduate students, I mean?" she asked.

"There are just nine so far—ten if you join us. There are more than that taking the degree course. I should say there'll be about forty in our department this year." Miss Mallory glanced at her wrist watch now and Janet took the hint and rose.

"I'll write for my transcript at Williston as soon as I get

home," she promised again earnestly. "And when that comes and you've gone over it, how long before I'll hear from you?"

Miss Mallory smiled. "You'll hear from me in about ten days after I get the record of your work," she replied.

Ten days! Janet wondered whether she could wait that long. But she would have to.

3

An Unexpected Encounter

SOMEHOW JANET PASSED THE TIME OF WAITING. There was an invitation to visit her former roommate, Ann Wickers, for a weekend up in the Thousand Islands, which she accepted. There was another weekend spent at the home of another classmate, who lived on the tip of Long Island. There was a delightful day with the home crowd at Jones Beach, on Long Island, a day that stretched into the late evening, because of the distance and in order that they could take in the musical show given there nightly. And there was always late tennis at the club, after her work at the Oakwood Hospital was over.

So the time went by without dragging too painfully. At last, the letter from Columbia-Presbyterian arrived, saying formally that her transcript had been received from Williston and the College of Physicians and Surgeons was happy to inform Janet Moore that she was eligible to enter their department of Physical Therapy for study for a Certificate of Proficiency in the coming September class. If she was still interested in so doing, would she kindly notify the di-

rector of her intentions, accompanying her letter with a
check for fifty dollars, which would be deducted from her
tuition upon payment of the full sum for the first term,
when she arrived at the college. A less formal note from
Miss Mallory was enclosed which read:

Dear Miss Moore,
    I suggest you come to see me as soon as convenient so
that we can arrange your schedule and also so that you com-
municate at once with the Registry of Off-Campus Accommo-
dations, 115 Livingston Hall, Columbia University, regarding
your living arrangements. I remember you said you would
prefer to be in an apartment, rather than in the dormitory at
Johnson Hall, and I have just heard that one is available, due
to a withdrawal of a prospective student.

    Janet did not write. She telephoned and made an ap-
pointment with the registry for the same day she was to
see Miss Mallory.

    It was the middle of August when Janet Moore entered
Miss Mallory's office for the second time and she felt a little
like a runner who has just won a long race.

    Miss Mallory, looking at her eager, triumphant face,
said, "You seem to be quite sure about wanting to do this
work you're getting into."

    "I am sure."

    "Why? What makes you feel that way?"

    Janet considered her answer carefully. . . . "Well, for one
thing, I like working with people. I didn't realize how
much until I did that volunteer work at the hospital at
home. I think—well—I think people are awfully interesting."

Miss Mallory nodded approvingly. "And you get along with them all right?"

"Oh, I didn't have any trouble—ever."

"Good! That's quite an asset. And you are strong physically, I would guess. That's essential, too."

"Mercy! I'm never sick."

"Even so, we require a physical examination of each of our students here," Miss Mallory told her. "That will be given later on, after classes begin. I might add in this connection that you are expected to learn how to swim, if you cannot already do so."

"I can swim."

Miss Mallory nodded a second time. "What about patience?" she asked smilingly. "Are you a patient person?"

Janet made a rueful face. "Well, I don't know as I'm famous for that. But I can learn to be, I believe."

"I'm sure you can, too. You have enough intelligence to realize that some things—like restoring injured and broken bodies to usefulness—take a long time. Now let's talk about your schedule for the first term. I have it roughly blocked out here to show what classes you will have to attend. Do you know you must carry seventeen points in nine courses?"

Janet raised an eyebrow. "That's one more than I carried Freshman year at Williston. But"—a smile crinkled up her freckled nose—"I'm a big girl now, so I guess I can take it. What are the subjects?"

"Anatomy for one. That comes three times a week. Exercise is another, twice a week. This gives you the theory and practice of basic movement. Twice a week, also, you'll have kinesiology, massage, medicine, and surgery—"

"Oh! That sounds interesting!"

"It is. Then there's neuroanatomy, which is the anatomy of the nervous system—"

"I know. I looked those up."

"—and nursing procedures—"

"That sounds interesting, too."

Miss Mallory smiled as she finished off the list. "There's also a course in orientation, which will teach you about professional ethics and institutional organization. And, last but not least, a course in physiology, two hours a week. How does it sound to you?"

Janet drew a deep breath. "Well—not easy exactly. Practically all sciences. And I wasn't a science major. I mean, I didn't get a B.S. degree."

"No, but I noticed on your transcript that the grades you received in your science courses were all good grades, so I don't think you'll have any trouble."

"I hope not!"

From Miss Mallory Janet went straight to the registry office. A little woman with white hair and glasses set on a thin nose greeted her. She was Mrs. Endicott.

"I'm glad you came in so quickly. We have rather an unusual situation on our hands. There were two students who arranged to take the last apartment we knew to be available. It's on 179th Street. But I heard, just a few days ago, that one of them is not coming because of ill health. The one who is coming—Kay Ferguson—wrote me that she would like to find another girl to share the expenses with her. Would you be interested? It's the only apartment left free and the rest of our incoming students have already made their arrangements. So, if you aren't interested, I shall have to try to place both you and Miss Ferguson elsewhere. How do you feel about it?"

Janet hesitated. What was the alternative? Johnson Hall. But she didn't want to live in a dormitory again. She was positive about that. Mrs. Endicott, seeing her uncertainty, broke in on her thoughts.

"I can get you a furnished room with a family where you would have to share the bathroom," she said.

There really isn't much choice, Janet told herself. It's too far for me to commute from Oakwood. So—

"Is this Miss Ferguson a Certificate student, too?" she asked.

"Yes, she's a graduate of a Midwestern college."

"Does she live anywhere near New York, so I could meet her before I decide?"

"I'm afraid not. Her home is in Missouri and she won't be coming on until college opens."

Janet made up her mind then quickly. "Well, it doesn't matter. I'll take the apartment with her, anyway. May I have her address, so I can write to her?" After all, she was thinking, she hadn't known anything about her Freshman roommate at Williston, either, yet that had worked out satisfactorily. This probably would, too.

She rose, expressed her thanks, and had reached the door before she remembered something else.

"By the way, what is the rent we have to pay?" she asked.

"One hundred and twenty dollars a month, I believe, although you had better check with the owner of the building, whose address I can give you. We have nothing to do with prices. That's between you and the owner or the agent."

"I see." Janet took the slip of paper on which Mrs. Endicott had written the address of the owner of the building where the two students were to live, spoke her thanks, and turned away.

That will be sixty dollars apiece, she was thinking as she went out, and with food—well—probably a hundred dollars a month would cover the total cost of her living expenses. Just about what Miss Mallory had told her.

In this way matters were settled. Janet Moore was admitted to the Physical Therapy department and she had a place to live. Now only a few weeks more and she would be started, she thought.

What would Dick Forsythe think of all this—if he knew?

The Oakwood Country Club was the only club in Oakwood. It was situated on a hill overlooking the valley where the town nestled. It had an eighteen-hole golf course, six tennis courts, and a large free-form swimming pool. The weekly dances in the great white-pillared building were popular with all ages, although certain dates were reserved particularly for certain groups.

The festivities this night in September were being held for the College Group. Those about to depart for a resumption of studies and those who had finished lately had gathered in large numbers. The Young Couples (Molly Evans and all her married friends) would have their turn later on and the Youth Circle—the high-school crowd—after that.

Janet was there. She went with Scott Murray, who was

to return to Princeton for his Senior year in a few days. She had known Scott all her life. They had gone through high school together, he always a year ahead of her, and the only reason he hadn't finished college before she did was because he had interrupted his course to put in two years in the Navy. At the time, he had thought he might not ever go back to Princeton. Indeed, one of the reasons why he had decided to do his stint in service when he did was because his marks were so low. But while he was in the Navy he had grown wiser and had determined he had better get his degree. He had been released last week and had come home with that determination unshaken. But, except for this strengthened purpose, he was much as he had always been.

He was good-looking, good-tempered, and good company. Easy-going. Janet liked him—as everyone did. If he was inclined to be casual about important matters, he was invariably excused, for he was ingratiating and pleasant. His low marks had been his own fault because he enjoyed fun more than work and did not take his responsibilities seriously.

He was humming now as he danced with Janet, and he was thinking somewhat lightly that she was a girl he could go for in a big way. As a matter of fact, he had given her a great deal of attention prior to his joining the Navy and prior to the appearance of Molly Evans' brother, Dick Forsythe, about whom he had heard but whom he had never met. Perhaps because of his own absence, Dick seemed to have gotten the inside track for a while. But now, Scott told himself, things were different—or could be. For one thing, he was home again, a free man. For another, he had heard rumors of a breakup between Janet and this Dick. How true were they? He hadn't been around long enough to find out but tonight seemed a good time to try.

He stopped his humming and held his partner off from him for a moment, scrutinizing her face. Same face, he told himself. Same sprinkle of freckles the color of her hair. Same hazel eyes. Same wide, generous mouth—

"Well?" She laughed. "Think you'll know me next time you see me?"

"Couldn't forget you, honey," he answered. "But that isn't the question."

"What is the question?"

He drew her a little closer and spoke into her ear. "I've heard tales of a cold war being waged between you and one Dick Forsythe. Is it still on?"

Janet's heart gave a lurch, as it always did when anyone brought up the subject of Dick Forsythe. She wished she'd get over that stupid reaction. And she might as well, for not once all summer had she heard a thing from him. Not that she had expected to—but, after all, he had a sister here in Oakwood with whom he had lived for several months last winter and to whom he was devoted. Surely he hadn't quarreled with her, so was it unreasonable to suppose that he might come to visit her occasionally and that she—Janet—might glimpse him in town once in a while? If that ever happened, what would she do? She had often wondered. How would she greet him? It would be ridiculous not to speak at all. She answered Scott a trifle constrainedly. "Yes, it's still on. Why?"

"Oh, I'm just thinking of my own future." His eyes

twinkled as they met hers. "You know me. Always looking out for myself. By the way, here's the punch bowl. Aren't you hot? Wouldn't you like a cooling drink?"

"Looking out for *me* this time, I suppose," Janet said mockingly. "Never a thought for you."

"Well, a second thought, maybe," he admitted, grinning at her. "One for you and two for me."

"I thought so. Listen, Scott. Let's sit awhile. After all, I played three sets of tennis today. I don't need more exercise."

"Choose your spot and I'll bring the cup that cheers to you. It'll take me awhile to fight through this crowd that's gathered around the board, so don't get impatient."

"I'll go out on the veranda. I'll be in the corner that looks over the swimming pool."

"Okay."

Scott nodded at her and began to push his way toward the punch bowl while Janet drifted to the long French doors. Outside were small groups, laughing and talking together, or couples murmuring quietly in shadowed places. Answering their tossed greetings, Janet made her way past them all, through the starlit darkness, to the far end of the porch, where there were a couple of lounge chairs near the steps that led down to the putting greens below and the pool next to them. Beyond the greens and the pool lay a grove of trees and beyond that, quite hidden from sight, a development of new homes.

She dropped into one of the chairs and put her head back. A half moon emerged from a vagrant cloud and spread light over the world, and it was then she saw him. Dick! Dick Forsythe! She sat bolt upright. He was coming up the steps, straight toward her. Her breath stopped and her bones seemed turned to water, while her thoughts raced. What was he doing here? He wasn't a member. Oh, of course. He had guest privileges through his sister Molly. He must have cut through the trees from her house on the other side of them. But what *was* he doing? Had he come to dance? And then he saw her and he halted in his tracks and spoke her name as if he had been running and were out of breath.

"Janet—!"

Somehow she recaptured her poise. She leaned back in her chair in the dress that echoed the color of her hair, looked up at him, and answered coolly, "Hello, Dick. Are you looking for someone?"

He moved toward her. "Yes, you. Molly told me you'd be here, so I came over."

Those broad, flat shoulders, that dark head poised so proudly, the caressing quality in his voice, of which he was so unconscious and which was always so endearing— But she stiffened herself against his power to move her and made no answer. She wasn't going to help him. Not one bit. If he had any reason for seeking her out, he could give it to her unaided. That moment of melting was over.

He towered above her. She could see his face now clearly. The familiar strong oblong of it, the firm mouth, the square chin, the dark eyes that could warm so tenderly or be so direct and demanding. They were demanding now.

"I want to talk to you."

"I really don't think we have anything to talk about."

With an abrupt movement, he reached down and jerked

the other chair around close to her and sat down on it, leaning forward with his elbows on his knees so that he could see her better.

"Janet! Don't be that way! There's too much at stake."

"There's nothing at all at stake."

"How can you say that—after those six months together?"

She looked straight at him. "Those six months ended. *You* ended them. Remember?"

"That's what I want to talk about."

There was urgency in his tone. He had known a long and lonely summer, during which he had had time to think many searching thoughts. For one thing, he blamed himself almost entirely for the break with Janet. He was older by four years and should have known enough to use persuasion, instead of opposition. That he hadn't was due to his surprise at learning she had no thought of marrying him—at least for quite awhile. It had really been a body blow to him, for in his mind it had been a settled thing for some time. And with the surprise had come anger and the feeling that she hadn't played quite fair with him.

There was, too, the belief that she was just voicing an impulsive, passing whim. After all, her life had lain in pleasant places. There was no pressure on her to earn money, so why this sudden desire to do so? And to take a whole year to fit herself for something when she didn't need to—when he could support her—when he was all ready to start their life together— He just hadn't been able to understand or fully believe her.

And then, when he had finally realized she was in earnest, he had offered what he had felt was a fair compromise. A job if she wanted it—yes—but nothing so important it would interfere with making their home the center of their lives, as Molly was doing with Brent and as his mother had done with his father. That was what marriage meant to him. But Janet would have none of it, and her aspirations were too vague to carry any weight with him. They were simply a completely unexpected obstacle to his own expectations and hopes. So he had spoken in haste and in heat—as she had, too—with the result that they had reached an end.

He said now, "I think we both said things at the inn without thinking."

"Maybe *you* did. I knew what I was saying the whole time."

He was silent, his dark eyes searching her face. This hardness in her was new to him, and he didn't know quite how to deal with it. Was it real? And lasting? Or a protective covering of some kind?

"The point is—" he began.

He was so close. His voice was so enveloping. She felt wrapped about by its tenderness. But this was weakness on her part. And where would it get her? Just to a yielding, to a capitulation in which all her plans would be upset or—worse yet—nullified. No. She had gone too far for that. He might as well realize it. She broke into his words.

"There isn't any point. You're having regrets a little too late. I've already decided what I'm going to do."

Rebuffed, he drew back. He was angered, too, for he had come tonight with an olive branch in his hand. But he controlled himself and, after a moment, he said, "I see. Will you tell me what it is?"

"Yes, if you really want to know."

"I do. I'm curious."

"I'm going to study Physical Therapy at Columbia University in New York. I've been accepted there and classes start next week." Her tone was firm. She heard it clearly and was proud that no wavering sounded in it because, in spite of the bitterness of her memories, seeing him now, being with him, talking with him, was bringing to an uncertain trembling life an old familiar magic.

He said slowly, "I told you you'd have to go back to school." He paused. "And after you finish, then what?"

"Then I'll get a job." She lashed out at him suddenly, unable to help herself in the turmoil of her emotions. *"You* have a job! Why shouldn't *I* have one, too?"

She saw his hands grip together. This talk wasn't going the way he had planned it. It was all no good and getting him nowhere. He stood up abruptly.

"Well, I guess there's no use in going over that argument any more. Only I'll tell you again that when I marry, I want a wife who is a wife and not a wage earner."

"You've already made that quite clear," she informed him. And then she added pointedly, "And now, if there's nothing more on your mind—?"

Dick stood immobile without speaking for a long moment, his eyes on the slender golden girl before him. He had blundered with his last words and he knew it. He had been dismissed and he knew that, too—but he knew also, in the same moment, that she could not dismiss him so easily. He had given her his love and he had not given it lightly. She did not want it now but the time could come—

after this year had passed—when she might feel different. About him. About marriage. About everything. He would wait.

He said, "That's all." Turning on his heel, he headed for the steps.

He was gone, swallowed up in the darkness of the trees below. She remained motionless in her chair, going over every word they had spoken together. What did they mean? What did they prove?

"Nothing," she said aloud. "Just nothing."

4

Orientation

THEY WERE TO MEET—all the new Physical Therapists, together with the Occupational Therapists—for Orientation,
and as Janet entered the amphitheater where they were
gathering, she was surprised at the number of them. Almost a hundred, she thought—and no one she knew at all!
If Kay Ferguson were here, as she was supposed to be,
Janet wouldn't even know her, since she hadn't an idea
as to what her new roommate looked like. And the only
other person at all familiar would be David Plunkett, who
might not remember her.

But he did. He was just inside the door as she came in
and he turned to speak to her with his white smile flashing
out of his tanned face.

"Hi! The clans are gathering, aren't they? How are
you?" he greeted her.

"I'm fine. And you?"

"Fine, too. Where are you living?"

"I'm in an apartment on 179th Street, with another girl.
Where are you?"

"In a little hole in the wall not far from my job."

"You have a job already?"

"Two. One through the day and one at night."

"What do you do?"

"I'm in the cafeteria in Presbyterian in the daytime and at night I'm a two-fingered typist for a doctor who's writing a book."

"Two-fingered?"

He grinned again. "Well, I wasn't asked if I used the touch system. I was just asked if I could type."

Janet said, "I had you figured out as a lifesaver at one of the beaches."

He looked surprised. "Well, I was that all summer, until Labor Day. How did you guess?"

Her glance touched his sun-bleached hair. "That—and your tan," she said. "But how are you going to work in the cafeteria all day after classes start?"

"I can't, of course. However, Miss Mallory has juggled my schedule so I'll have part time there, anyway. You working your way, too?"

Janet shook her head, and then his eyes swept her quickly from head to foot. She was dressed in a pale green suit with a fragile white blouse and white accessories and a single strand of pearls about her throat, and the effect was one of expensive simplicity. "No, I guess not," he added.

Just then, Miss Mallory spoke from the front of the room where she was standing. "Now, if the rest of you who have still not found seats will please do so—"

There was movement and the scraping of chairs and Janet and Dave took places next to each other in the last row. A silence fell and Miss Mallory spoke again.

"Ladies and gentlemen, welcome to you all. I'm very proud of the large number of you this year." And she smiled approvingly at them before going on. "We have met here today in order to hear a few words from Dr. Dearborn, the chairman of the Department of Physical Medicine and Rehabilitation. May I introduce to you Dr. Dearborn?"

A slender, gray-haired man rose from the front row of chairs. His glasses glittered in the light that fell on him while he waited for the small rustling sounds to subside. His voice was quiet and full of seriousness, yet held a genuine warmth as he greeted the therapists and then went on to his main subject.

"You are here this morning to be given an introduction to a very specialized profession within the medical field— rehabilitation. I should like to explain to you first that rehabilitation has a philosophy. It is the affirmation of the right of every human being to as healthy and full a life as possible. That is our philosophy. And our aim is the ultimate restoration of the disabled person to his maximum capacity—physical, emotional, social, and vocational." He paused a moment before continuing. His audience was very quiet and attentive!

"As you know, some people are born with faulty nerves or muscles or with a brain that does not get its messages straight. Some have had accidents—perhaps a fall, a car collision, or a shallow dive. And some have had an operation or a disease such as arthritis or multiple sclerosis. Still others have been involved in a war and have returned from it with crippling injuries. All of these people need help to enable them to return to a life of usefulness. They need *your* help, the help of both physical therapists and occupational therapists. For you work as a team, with each other and with many others. I want to emphasize that. You work with nurses, with speech therapists, with neurologists, with orthopedists, with vocational counselors, with social workers, with psychiatrists. And always, *always* you work under a physician's orders. The important thing is that you are working together as a team and toward the same end." He paused again.

"All kinds of people," he went on, "in all age groups of both sexes and all nationalities and races are treated by you. There is no discrimination, any more than there is discrimination in the admission of qualified students in our classes. We treat all kinds and we take all kinds to help in the treatments. For that reason, ours is a unifying profession. It is also a heart-warming profession because it meets a vital human need."

Janet whispered to Dave, "He's really giving us a good bird's-eye view of things, isn't he?" And Dave nodded in agreement.

"I will not this morning go into details about the way you will work," Dr. Dearborn continued. "Or about the kinds of things you will do and will help your patients to do. You will learn all that in your courses. I will simply say briefly that, as students, you will study the workings and design of the human body, in anatomy, pathology, psychology, and physiology. You will also learn to measure and test patients, so you can evaluate their conditions. Much of the teaching you will receive will take place in a laboratory where, in small groups, you will participate in direct clinical practice under the eyes of your instructors.

"But this morning I chiefly want you to realize the great importance of the work you are undertaking. It may surprise you to be told that rehabilitation traces its roots back to the ancient Greeks and Romans. It took a long time for it to be recognized as a phase of medical care. And it did not begin to grow up until World War Two. Since then, the importance of rehabilitation as an allied service to medicine—as the third phase after prevention and treatment, the phase that takes a patient from his bed to a job —has been increasingly recognized by medical doctors and other health authorities all over the country."

He cleared his throat, then went on with his talk.

"When we began our services toward the end of World War Two, there were more than 2,000 American soldiers with both legs paralyzed. Of these over 1,700 now live in their own homes and drive their own cars. And at least 1,500 of them are earning their own living. We are proud, indeed, of our record in helping these unfortunate men. But we are prouder of the way our services have grown, for now we cannot only help victims of war but also victims of strokes, cerebral palsy, blindness, fractures, amputations, and various diseases.

"As a result, the demand for therapists exceeds the supply. Today, there are 5,000,000 people needing rehabilitation help. Within the next decade, 30,000 new physical therapists will be needed. And the demand for occupational therapists is even greater. There are, in other words, more positions open than can be filled. What I am saying to you in all earnestness is that we *need* you. We need you badly. And so we welcome you most happily as you meet with us today. And we hope you will find the work you are to do both interesting and inspiring, as we believe it to be."

He was finished. Janet joined in the round of applause but she was a little stunned by all that she had heard. She had had no idea of the scope of the work done, and that record of restoring so many American soldiers to usefulness was almost unbelievable. If, in time, she could help one person—just *one*—

Her thoughts were cut short by Miss Mallory, who took the floor again to introduce Miss Dickson. And now Miss Dickson was explaining where in the great, sprawling Medical Center the work laboratories for the students would be located—in the Vanderbilt Clinic, on the Orthopedic floor in Presbyterian Hospital and in the Neurological Institute, a separate building across Fort Washington Avenue.

"You all have your schedules by now," she concluded. "And you will be expected to report to your first class the day after tomorrow. I might add that no cuts are allowed, so you will be expected to report to *all* your classes every single day. And now, if you have any questions—?" There were a few and she answered them before she finished. "Before you all leave, may I remind the physical therapists to come to Miss Mallory's office this afternoon for a social hour, in order for you to meet your future instructors. Tomorrow, as you know, is your last free day before classes so—enjoy yourselves! That is all."

Janet waited until the last student left the amphitheater, hoping that she would discover her roommate, someone who would be looking for her as she was looking for Kay

Ferguson. But everyone was moving out in little groups of twos and threes and she seemed to be the only person alone. She told Dave she would not lunch in the cafeteria. Instead, she thought she would go back to her apartment, just in case Kay had arrived too late for the meeting and had gone up there. And with a nod and a smile she left him.

Janet was already familiar with her new quarters. Kay had written her that their rent was paid for two months in advance and Janet could get a key from the owner of the building and move in any time after the fifteenth of September that she wanted. So she had secured the key and Scott had driven her in to the city in his car, with her two large suitcases and a couple of hatboxes, before he left for Princeton. He had carried everything up the one flight of stairs for her except her coats, which she had carried, and then had poked around to see what the place was like.

"*Hhm.* Not elegant exactly. Not what you could call sumptuous. But, I suppose, adequate," he had said.

Adequate was the word. It was on the second floor and looked over 179th Street. You entered directly into a small living room, large enough to hold a drop-leaf table flanked by two straight chairs, two tired-looking easy chairs upholstered in a despondent brown, one standing lamp, and an empty bookcase with an open front. There was a coat closet at one end of the room, a cheap and badly worn figured rug in all colors on the varnished floor, a wavy mirror on the tan wall above the drop-leaf table, and a wall telephone. Opening off this room at the rear was a tiny kitchen and next to that the bathroom. In the kitchen the fixtures, including the gas stove, were old, the paint was chipped off the refrigerator, and the sink stained. Above the sink on either side were cupboards for what dishes there were—a collection of unmatched pieces—and below the sink were stacked the pots and pans, in another cupboard. The bathroom had a tub on four legs with a shower rigged up above it. There was no shower curtain.

Across a small hall were two bedrooms, both with pale cream walls and each furnished exactly like the other, with a single divan for a bed, a flat-top desk, a brown bureau, and one straight chair. If there had ever been curtains anywhere, there were none there at the moment, although there were good cream-colored shades at all the windows.

"Adequate—and no more," Janet had murmured to Scott in agreement. Yet it was just what you could expect for a setup meant to rent to different college students each year. She remembered clearly how her rooms at Williston had looked until she had introduced her own personal possessions, thus adding color and individuality to drabness. She could do the same thing here, she had thought, and her mind had begun planning how to improve the place, but she had decided to wait until she met Kay, who might have ideas, too.

She approached the apartment today with hopeful excitement rising in her heart and ran up the flight of stairs a little breathlessly. Would Kay Ferguson, indeed, be here? What would she be like? Would she be easy to get along with? Would she be neat or sloppy? Would she enjoy doing half the cooking? Would she, above all, want to make

their living quarters more attractive or wouldn't she care
how the place looked?

Janet reached the top step. Yes, someone was here. She
could see at once that this was so because their entrance
door stood wide and just inside there was an unopened
suitcase standing on the floor. As Janet went in, a girl,
dressed all in brown, turned from the front window to
face her.

She was small and dark, with a round face and round,
bright brown eyes. *Elfish* was the word that sprang to
Janet's mind. Quick-moving, with a mop of short brown
curly hair and a dimple high on one cheek when she
smiled, she had, indeed, an elfish charm about her. She
spoke now in an unexpectedly deep voice that held a warm
friendliness.

"You must be Janet Moore. I was watching for you out
of the window. My train was late, so I came straight up
here. I only arrived here about five minutes ago."

"I guessed that was what had happened."

"Did I miss anything important?"

"I'll tell you later." Janet spoke with a sudden rush.
"Look, Kay. I didn't know which bedroom to take but
they were just alike and the same size, so I couldn't see
that one was any better than the other. I've moved into
the farthest one. Okay?"

"Oh, of course."

Janet went on. "I laid in some food for us, too—a little.
Enough for our supper tonight and breakfast in the morning."

"Good! I'll settle with you for that."

"And I've got to settle with you because you advanced the rent for two months."

"Also twenty dollars toward the gas and electricity." Kay gestured and her dimple appeared. "But don't worry about it. We'll work things out. We'll get a system going. A kitty, maybe, for food. And—" She gestured again, with a quick dismissing wave of her hand. "We'll work things out all right." She dropped now into one of the brown upholstered chairs, kicked off her pumps, and curled up like a small child. Then her glance went around the room in a kind of secret merriment and she said demurely, "So this is Paradise."

Janet laughed aloud and dropped into the other chair. "Do you think we can improve on it? Add harps or something?"

And with those few words rapport was immediately established between them.

5

A Free Day

W HEN DO YOU THINK HE'LL GET HERE?" Kay asked Janet.

"Mother said about eleven this morning," Janet replied.
"Why?"

"Well, I have to go pay my fees at the office and I want
to get back before he comes. I don't want to miss any of
the excitement."

"You'll have time. It's only nine-thirty now."

It was the day after Kay's arrival and the girls were both
having coffee at the drop-leaf table in the living room.
Janet looked down at her thick white cup now and made
a face.

"I'm so glad I remembered about my fiesta ware that I
had at college," she said.

They had spent the evening before making plans to
beautify their apartment. Neither of them wanted to spend
much money to get stuff they would in all probability
leave behind at the end of the year, and while they were
pondering that problem Janet had an inspiration.

"Our third floor!" she had exclaimed.

"What about your third floor?"

"Why, we've got a maid's room up there all furnished—and no maid any more. Now we have a cleaning woman by the day and we send out the laundry and when my parents give dinner parties, Mother and Dad either take their guests to the club or have in a couple who specialize in serving dinners. So there's a room full of things up there that I'm sure Mother will let us borrow."

"Neat! But how'll we get it all in to the city?"

"Oh, that's easy. There's a Tim O'Brien in Oakwood who's an odd job man. He'll do anything—anything at all. And he has a truck." Janet had jumped up. "I'll telephone Mother right away and ask her about it. She can call Tim for us."

So Janet had done just that, and her mother had said of course they could have the things, and what, exactly, did they want? Janet had answered that she remembered a little table up there and wasn't there a lamp of some kind? And what about a rug? She thought it was a plain tan job and would her mother mind taking a look and getting the measurements of it and then call her back because the rug was terribly important. It would—could—make or break the whole scheme. She might list what else was there, too, if she would. Meanwhile, she and Kay would make a list—

It had been a busy evening. Janet kept thinking of her own possessions that could be brought from her room at home. Her little radio, her desk lamp, a small chair or two— And then came the question of curtains.

"Those I guess we'll have to buy," Kay had said. "But we can get cheap ones."

Janet had agreed and had measured the length and width of the windows with a ruler.

"There's a dry-goods store in Oakwood. When Mother calls back, I'll ask her if she could manage to go there and get something inexpensive for us before Tim drives in here. I think she'd have time, if she's free. Let's see. There are three windows here and we each of us has a window in her bedroom—that's five pair. Now what about the kitchen?"

"Oh, why not let that go for now? There must be a Five-and-Ten in this neighborhood where we can pick up something later on."

"Right."

So when Mrs. Moore telephoned a little later she and her daughter compared lists and together evolved a "master list," as Janet called it. And—yes—Mrs. Moore had been able to get in touch with Tim, who was free the next day and would take the job. And—yes—she would be glad to see about the curtains. She said that these would be her donation to the new home because, when the girls were through with them, she was sure she could use them somewhere herself.

Now Janet said, "I only wish we didn't have to go to that luncheon the Seniors are giving us today."

"I don't understand just who are Seniors," Kay answered.

"The degree students who are starting their second year are Seniors. I imagine we are, too, we Certificate students. But being new here, we're guests today, not hostesses."

"I see. Well, I wish, too, we didn't have to take time to go to that luncheon when we have so much to do here."

"The thing is, it's a custom. It's done every year. And that Dorothy Drake was so nice, I don't see how we can get out of it. She's the Senior who was helping at the tea party in Miss Mallory's office yesterday afternoon when we met our future instructors. She particularly said she'd be looking for us."

Kay nodded resignedly. "By the way, what about that Dave Plunkett you introduced to me at that tea? He seems to me to be terribly gone on you."

Janet looked astonished. "Don't be silly," she said. "I've just met him. I've only seen him three times in my life."

"All the same, he's gone."

"Don't be silly," Janet repeated.

"Well, all right, but listen. I heard him asking Miss Dickson—I think it was Miss Dickson—how much a P.T. graduate could expect to be paid on his first job. And when she told him between $3,800 and $4,800 he said, 'Do you think two people can live on that?'"

"So—?"

"So then Miss Dickson laughed and answered that two people could, of course, especially if the second person was a P.T., too. And I saw him look over at you and grin and say that was an idea. And thanks, he'd remember it."

Janet shrugged. "He's a nice person. I like him. *But—*"

Kay's bright brown eyes looked at her inquiringly. "But you've somebody else in mind who means more, maybe?"

Janet shook her head. She and Kay were going to room together all year and probably, in time, they'd exchange confidences but right now Janet had no desire to say anything about Dick Forsythe. Why should she, anyway? He was out of her life.

"Nobody," she answered firmly. And then—"What about you?"

"Oh, I'm free as air. Though, to tell you the truth, I wish I weren't. I'd like to be engaged. I really would."

"Honestly?"

"Honestly. I can't think of anything nicer than getting married."

"What are you taking this course for, then?"

"In case I don't have any luck. And because Mother and Dad think I ought to be able to earn my own living, come what may. I suppose it's a good idea, too."

"Yes, it's a good idea," Janet agreed. "Besides which"—thoughtfully—"we're terribly needed, as I found out yesterday. But hey! You'd better be on your way, if you want to get down to the University office and back by eleven."

Tim was late in arriving. It was after twelve o'clock when Janet spied his truck at the curb below, so that there was only time for him to carry everything up to their apartment before the girls had to go on to the luncheon.

"What a mess!" Kay exclaimed, after he was gone and she stood looking at the litter he had left in the living room. "And we can't do a single thing about it till we get back."

"We'll come back early," Janet declared. "And let's not forget to stop on the way and pick up some food for our dinner tonight."

"We might stop and see about some kitchen curtains, too. Shall we?"

"Okay. What's your idea about them?"

"Well, something cute and gay. We'll know when we

see what's there. It's a good thing we have this free day in which to get settled, isn't it?"

"Free—yet not free, so not nearly long enough. Well, come on. The sooner we get there, the sooner we can leave."

The luncheon was strictly a student affair. The minute Janet and Kay entered Residence Hall they were spotted and greeted by Dorothy Drake, a pudgy, cheerful blonde, they had met the day before in Miss Mallory's office. Immediately pinning name tags on their left shoulders for identification purposes, she began leading them around to introduce them to everyone.

"I don't see David Plunkett," Kay said in an aside to Janet.

"He's probably working in the cafeteria today," Janet answered. "This affair isn't really a *must*. It's a courtesy thing."

It proved to be an unexpectedly interesting hour, Janet thought, for here Dr. Dearborn's words were proven right. Not only were there men taking this course but there were also people of all nationalities and color. A young Negro had a place next to her at the long luncheon table. A Japanese girl sat opposite. And a Filipino, a Greek, and an East Indian were farther along. It was almost like being in International House.

It was interesting, too, because of all the assorted facts that Dorothy, who sat between Janet and Kay, told them. During the course of the meal, Janet happened to ask her what she planned to do when she finished her clinical work next fall. The question brought forth a flood of information as Dorothy laid down her fork to answer.

"It's hard for me to decide," she said. "Of course, I have a whole year yet but I've done a lot of thinking. There are so many ways to go that I'm finding it difficult to know which one I want to take."

"I didn't realize that," Janet said. "What are some of the ways?"

"Well, in the first place, I'll have to get more experience after I finish my training. You always have to do that. So I think I'll go into a hospital here in New York for a year or two—maybe three. After that—" She held up her hand and checked off her fingers as she spoke. "One—I could teach. Two—I could aim for a supervisory job. Three—there's research, though that doesn't appeal to me very much."

"You mean teach in a college or university? Physiology or anatomy or something like that?"

Dorothy nodded. "In a Physical Therapy department, of course—either as a regular instructor, working up to a professorship, or as a clinical instructor, going around with the students to the different areas and explaining to them what's going on. You'll be going around with a clinical instructor next term yourself and you'll see then what I mean," she finished.

Kay now leaned around from the other side of Dorothy to ask a question in her turn. "What about P.T's in the armed services?" she queried. "Are they ever used there?"

"I should say so! The Air Force, the Army, and the Navy offer commissions to women P.T's. I've thought of that, too, I admit."

"I wonder what it would be like to serve in one of the branches?" Kay murmured speculatively.

"She's husband-hunting," Janet explained laughingly. "What she's really asking you is whether or not one of the armed services would be good hunting ground."

Kay made a face at her. "I am not!" she returned indignantly. "I'm curious about salaries and things like that."

Dorothy smiled at both of them. "Oh, as to salaries and benefits and quarters' allowances—they're very good, I believe. And comparable in all three services. If you like military life—" She looked at Kay questioningly. "Do you?"

"I don't know. I've never tried it."

"Well, if you think you'd like it, I would say an officer's commission opens up a really solid career. You would be a second lieutenant or an ensign, you know, right from the start."

Kay nodded. "I might get to see the world that way."

"You might."

"And"—put in Janet—"you might find a husband, too." She turned to Dorothy. "But do you have any ideas about what *you* are going to do after your three years in a hospital?"

"As I told you, I'm really not sure yet. I'm thinking, though, quite seriously, about going into Public Health. The United States Government has a Public Health Commission Corps that is open to women as well as men and it has rank, pay, and benefits, just as in the armed services."

"Well! Am I learning things!" Janet exclaimed. "I've been pretty stupid, I guess. It never occurred to me to find out what openings this profession might have or what my first job would pay or whether there'd be many opportunities—whether the field was crowded or not, I mean. Yes, I've been pretty stupid. Well! Excuse me for interrupting you, Dorothy. Go on and tell us, please, what, exactly, you would do in Public Health?"

"I'd do a lot of things," Dorothy answered. "I'd be working under the Department of Health, Education and Welfare. That department treats the sick, does research into the cause, prevention, and cure of diseases, gives assistance technically and financially to states to help them improve their health programs—" She paused for breath and Janet said approvingly, "You've learned the answers very well. Go to the head of the class."

Dorothy laughed. "Well, I found out all about it because I really think I'd like to make that my chosen field. I'd like to end up as a consultant, I think. Oh, yes! One thing more. This corps is responsible for the health care of both the Coast Guard and the Merchant Marine. Or did I tell you that?"

"No, but you've told us enough to start us planning ahead, too," Janet said. "I'm quite dizzy thinking of all I can do when I graduate. Does the Physical Therapy Association have a placement service to help you get your first job?"

"Oh, yes," Dorothy answered. "Of course."

Kay said now, "You've made it all sound awfully glamorous, somehow, I think."

"Glamorous?" Dorothy's cheerful, chubby face turned serious. "Yes, it can be that. But don't forget that a glamorous assignment usually means working under difficult conditions that call for adaptability and—well—ingenuity, sometimes. For example, you might be asked to set up a

Physical Therapy department in a hospital in a South American country where it's hot and living conditions are anything but luxurious and you have no equipment. Or you might be called to a foreign country for emergency duty in an epidemic. Only a few years ago six P.T's were sent by the American Red Cross to Morocco to help rehabilitate the 10,000 people there who had been stricken by paralysis, due to contaminated cooking oil."

"Really? Did P.T's do that?" Kay and Janet both exclaimed.

"They certainly did. What's more, there's to be a P.T. school set up in Nigeria soon, I believe, where there has never been one before in the whole country. England has given a grant for its establishment. Do you want to go to Nigeria?" Suddenly, Dorothy looked down at her plate. "Goodness! I haven't taken a bite! Let me live in the present instead of the future for a few moments and enjoy this meal, will you? Suppose you two talk while I eat. Tell me what you're going to do the rest of your free day when this party is over."

"What are we going to *do!*" they chorused together. And then Janet said, "Come and see us some time soon and we'll show you what we're going to do. Or, rather, what we will have done."

"I'll start in the kitchen while you work in the living room."

"All right, Kay, if you want it that way. But you've picked the dirtiest job. And I'm going to need some help here with the rug soon."

"Call me when you're ready."

The girls had come back from the luncheon, not forgetting to stop at the delicatessen and to purchase the
kitchen curtains. Now they had changed to their shorts and
were ready to create order out of the chaos Tim had left
in his wake. Looking at it, Janet exclaimed, "Honestly!
What a mess! And what a pile of work for us to do! Were
we dumb? Or weren't we?"

"We weren't. Just wait." Kay disappeared into the
kitchen. A moment later, Janet heard water running, the
sound of a pail banging against a faucet, pots and pans
rattling, and dishes clattering. Above it came Kay's voice.
"Boy! *Everything* has got to be scrubbed!" She groaned,
then added, "I'll swap rooms with you, Jan!"

"No, you won't! You chose that place!" Janet answered
promptly and she began to move things out of the living
room into the tiny hall. A table, two chairs, a standing
lamp, some cartons, and a number of boxes— Goodness!
What was in them all? There simply wasn't room enough
out there to move everything. She would have to shove the
two big easy chairs and the drop-leaf table toward one end
of the room. Then she'd unroll the rug, that now stood
up in a corner, as far down to those pieces as she could
get and call Kay to help her lift the furniture back over
it, so she could unroll the rest. Oh, if only Tim hadn't
been late and could have helped with this much, at least!
But there was no use moaning over that now.

So Janet pulled and she heaved and she hauled, until the
room was cleared of the small stuff that Tim had brought
and the three big pieces that belonged here were pushed
against the two front windows. She did hope the rug from
home would entirely cover up the worn ornate job that

was on the floor already. If she'd measured correctly—and her mother had, too—

Tugging at the roll, she flopped it to the floor and then eased it around until it lay even with the old carpet. Good! There were two inches to spare on the width. Now for the length. Pushing with both hands, she unrolled it until it touched the chairs. Then she called for Kay.

"What do you want?" Kay called back. "I'm busy! I'm up to my ears in soapsuds! Can't you get along?"

Well, she could try.

The upholstered chairs with their wide arms were clumsy to get hold of and terribly heavy, but there wasn't much of a hump to lift them over, so Janet managed. She got the table against the wall again and she put the two easy chairs opposite it, facing each other. Then she finished unrolling the rug and stood back to survey the result. Joy! The old floor covering was completely hidden and the place looked better already.

Encouraged, she moved quickly to other tasks. She took down the wavy mirror and tucked it against the wall, way in the back of the closet. She opened a box and found two stretch slip covers that she fitted over the upholstered chairs. She unpacked books—and some pictures—a bowl or two—a couple of candleholders— Oh, here was the box containing the curtains. How perfect! But—*rods,* she thought suddenly. They'd forgotten about curtain rods! She glanced up at the windows in dismay—and there the needed fixtures were—just waiting. Luck!

Janet could hear Kay in the kitchen, banging around, and once Janet pushed in to her through the door the carton that held all the gay fiesta ware. But Kay called to her, "Keep out! Keep out till I'm through!" So Janet withdrew, saying only, "There's another carton or two marked 'For the kitchen,' but you can come and get them when you're ready for them."

Both girls worked the balance of the afternoon and up until midnight, forgetting all about eating supper. When at last they stopped, they were dead tired—and starved. But what a transformation had been worked in those few hours! They could hardly believe their own eyes.

The living room was delightful, with its spotless tan carpet, tan walls, and pale green slip covers over the ugly brown of the easy chairs. There was a low, round table between the chairs, with a green bowl in the middle of it holding artificial marigolds. Where the wavy mirror had been an oil painting of a wood scene in fall colors of flame and rust and gold and green hung. Tailored cream-colored curtains of net hung at the windows. Green candles in two brass holders stood at either end of the bookcase, with the radio between them. Books with bright bindings partly filled the shelves and over the whole scene lay the subdued light from three lamps.

"Oh, Jan!" Kay murmured.

"Good?"

"Paradise now. Now come see my kitchen."

A red rubber mat concealed the worn spot in the black-and-white linoleum in front of the sink. Beside this, on the shelf, stood a red rubber dish drainer. Two red-handled pots hung against the wall, next to the stove, while two red dish towels were suspended from a rod on the back of the door. The cupboard above the sink was open and all Janet's red and yellow fiesta ware twinkled there, the plates in neat piles, the cups dangling from brass hooks. At the one window there was a crisp red-and-white checked gingham curtain.

"It's all clean," Kay said. "That's what took the time."

"I'll bet."

"But it still needs a coat of paint everywhere."

"Which it won't get tonight."

"Or ever, probably."

They went to the refrigerator and took out a package of ham slices and another of cheese and made themselves sandwiches. Then they opened a couple of bottles of ginger ale. Finally, they carried their plates and their bottles and their two glasses into the living room, put them on plastic mats on the little round table, and sank into the easy chairs with great sighs of satisfaction.

"We weren't dumb, you see," Kay said.

"No, we were quite bright."

"You were, anyway. You knew just what to tell your mother to send. I like that squatty bronze lamp you've put on the table. Your mother sent that, didn't she?"

"*Mm.*" Janet spoke with her mouth full. Presently, she said, "Mother sent a shower curtain, too, but I'm too tired to put it up."

"It can wait." There was silence while Kay munched on her sandwich. Then—"The bathroom doesn't need anything but that."

"A bathmat. Mother sent one. It's white, like the shower curtain." She sighed. "There are a few more things that I haven't found places for yet—but I will."

More silence. Glasses clinked on plates. Bottles were emptied. The last crumb was eaten.

"There isn't much to do to our bedrooms," Janet said in a voice of utter contentment. "My gold couch cover from college—the little yellow boudoir chair that Tim brought from my room at home—a new yellow desk blotter, and my yellow desk lamp, and I'm fixed. Oh, and curtains. Just like these in here. It won't take long."

"And my couch cover—a blue one—is in my trunk that's coming. And I'll get a new desk blotter, too. Blue." Kay put her head back and her brown eyes were dreamy. "Oh, Jan! We've made a home. A real home! My first one. Hasn't it been fun?"

Janet nodded slowly, a little surprised at herself because she remembered she hadn't wanted to make a home for Dick—not at all! But it had, indeed, been fun.

6

❀

The First Week

Physical therapy," Dr. Beaton was saying, "deals with the prevention, correction, and alleviation of disease and injury by using manual and other means and devices according to the prescription of a physician."

Janet thought, I don't need to write that down. I know it now.

This was the first class on Janet's schedule. Kay was seated next to her on one side and on the other was the little Japanese girl—Mitsu Something-or-other. Janet had seen David's blond head way in the back of the room as she entered.

Dr. Beaton continued, "From this definition it is not hard to deduce our objectives. We aim to eliminate or lessen the patient's disability as far as possible and to retrain him to live and work within the limits of his disability to his utmost capacity."

Beside her, Janet felt Mitsu stir slightly and she wondered if her classmate was having any trouble understanding what was being said. She tried to imagine herself going to Japan with only a little knowledge of the language and sitting in on a lecture like this, where long, hard, technical words were used. It would be difficult, she thought.

"To achieve our objectives," Dr. Beaton said, "we use light, heat, water, and electricity. We use skill in massage. We use therapeutic exercise. Exercise is most frequently used. For that reason, we are meeting here today so that you can begin the study of the anatomy of the human body."

Mitsu stirred again, and Janet turned to smile at her. The Japanese girl smiled back and Janet thought, She's pretty. If she has any trouble, maybe I can help her. Then she returned to Dr. Beaton's words.

"—The bones and the related structures are called collectively the skeletal system. The joints are known as the articulatory system. Then there is the muscular system, with which we will be particularly concerned. There will be lectures and there will be laboratory work, with prepared dissection."

"Ooh!" Kay whispered. "I didn't know about that!"

Dr. Beaton's glance turned toward the whisper and Kay bent her head over her textbook. Janet wrote a note and pushed it unobtrusively toward her friend.

"He said 'prepared.' It's not bad. Nothing bloody. The dissection is all done for us before we get to the lab. Miss Mallory told me."

The lecture went on. Janet took rapid notes. She noticed that Mitsu simply listened, every once in a while turning her head to smile shyly out of her bright black eyes. As the class ended and they all moved to leave the room, Janet spoke to the Japanese student.

"Is it hard for you to understand?"

Mitsu nodded. "A leetle," she admitted. "But I shall study *vairy* good."

"If I can help you any time—"

Mitsu's smile spread over her whole face. "Oh, thank you! You are mos' kind!"

Kinesiology. Miss Smith was lecturing. "Kinesiology is the science which studies human motion and our aim is to understand how the human machine works. The word kinesiology comes from a Greek verb *kinesi,* which means movement or motion. Now, motion is produced by muscle movement and is not a single isolated process. The nervous system, the circulatory and respiratory and digestive systems all play their part in movement."

Janet's pen flew. Miss Smith talked so fast!

"The human body," the instructor went on, "is a self-propelling machine, with the power supplied by muscle contraction. Every muscle has two ends attached to different bones and we will study the origin and attachments of *all* these muscles."

Whew! Janet thought. That's a large order.

Orientation. And Miss Mallory went on to explain about the desirable professional attitudes that should be developed by Physical Therapists.

"In the first place," she said with emphasis, "remember always that you work only under a doctor's orders. You never diagnose. You never prescribe treatment. Nor do you ever question a doctor's words to doubt them, only to understand them. Neither do you ever discuss a patient's condition before him or before other patients—or, for that matter, before anybody else. What you know or learn about your patients is strictly confidential."

She paused to let her words sink in.

"Another important thing," she continued, after a moment, "is remembering that your patient is a person—a person and not just a disease. He or she is a person with feelings—and you must respect those feelings. You must never fail, when preparing a patient for treatment, to allow him his personal dignity, his sense of privacy. I cannot emphasize that too much.

"Naturally," she went on, "you should enjoy working with people, for you will be teachers a great deal of the time. You teach your patients what to do. You teach them how to use braces, crutches, and other prosthetic helps. You also teach parents of children and relatives of adults how to continue exercises at home. You will have to learn to coax, tease, or command in your teaching, in order to accomplish your purpose, which is—always—*to get the patient to start helping himself.* For all this you will need endless patience and understanding. Finally, you must never fail in optimism and cheerfulness."

When Janet reached their apartment that night with Kay, she dropped down in one of the easy chairs and looked questioningly at her friend, who had dropped down in the other chair.

"The first day is over. How do you think it's going to be?"

"Tough," Kay answered promptly. "Kinesiology—all those muscles to learn—wow!"

"Yes, but I think the dissection in the anatomy lab will help there," Janet said thoughtfully, and Kay nodded in agreement. "By the way, did you know that, after today, we go down to the Institute for the Crippled and Disabled, on Twenty-third Street and First Avenue, for our class in Massage? They have little rooms there where we can practice whatever we learn on each other. We're to have both Massage and Exercise down there, I think."

"Yes, I know."

"Nursing Procedures is going to be interesting, I imagine," Janet went on. "It's so practical. Bandaging and dressings and first aid and bedside conduct—" She broke off. "Bedside conduct," she repeated. *"All* our conduct, for that matter! Remember when Miss Mallory was talking to us about desirable personable qualifications for Physical Therapy?"

"Uh-huh."

"She made it sound as though we had to be just about everything perfect." Janet opened her notebook and found a certain page. "Listen!" And she read aloud, "Personal qualifications needed for Physical Therapists are good health, energy reserve, emotional balance and maturity, cooperativeness, poise, friendliness, insight, and sympathetic understanding." She closed her notebook and looked across at Kay. "Do you suppose we're all of that?" she asked.

And Kay, laughing, answered, "Why, we must be! We were accepted for this course, weren't we?"

The next few days went by swiftly. The girls had their physical examinations and learned then that, if they were ever ill and required hospitalization, they would be taken care of in Medical Center. They thought that was nice to know—but neither expected to be sick at any time, of course.

They were also given their uniforms and were told they were not required to wear these until the spring term, when they must put them on for Clinical Observation. The uniforms were one-piece white dresses. They were short-sleeved and buttoned to the waist, with snaps all the way down the skirt so that they could be opened easily. The skirt had one big pocket on the right side. There was a white insignie sewed high on the left sleeve. This had the words *Columbia University* circled around it, with the letters P.T. in the center. Each girl was given three of these uniforms, in a size that fitted her. They were hung carefully in the closets for future use.

By now, Janet and Kay had attended, at least once, all of their classes, and they were well aware that this first term was going to require some hard study on their part. But they had become so interested in the courses that related practically to Physical Therapy—the Exercise Course of Basic Movement, the course in Massage and Techniques of Relaxation, and the one in Nursing Procedures—that they had readily accepted the necessity for mastering the other theoretical courses.

By now, too, they had learned their way around the different parts of the huge Medical Center and how to use the short cut, via the underground tunnel, to the Neurological Institute. They knew where the Libraries were and the University Bookstore and the Secondhand Bookshops which were not far from the Columbia campus. They had also discovered that there were different clubs they could join if they cared to—all kinds of clubs, covering all kinds of interests—but for the present both girls decided to join nothing. They thought they would be busy enough with their studies, the things they wanted to do and see in the city, short visits to Janet's home in Oakwood or elsewhere, and the little parties they planned to give in their refurbished apartment.

Janet had found one other way to fill her time. She had been so disappointed to discover that she would have no direct contact with patients before the second term that she went to Miss Mallory about it.

"I have part of two afternoons free," she said to her. "Wouldn't it be possible for me to spend some of that time just visiting around and watching what's going on in the different areas?"

Miss Mallory considered the question. "It's not usual," she answered after a moment. "Don't you think you'll need those hours for study? Most students do."

"A lot of students take their spart time to earn money," Janet pointed out. "I don't need to do that." And she waited.

"Well," Miss Mallory said slowly, "if you'd like, you might go around with Dorothy Drake, who is getting her clinical experience here in Presbyterian this term. You wouldn't wear a uniform and you wouldn't do anything, not anything at all. You would simply observe."

"Oh, but that would be wonderful!" Janet exclaimed. "That's what I want to do. Will you speak to Dorothy about it?"

"Yes. I will."

So it was arranged. And the very next day Janet met Dorothy in the cafeteria and had lunch with her, following which the two of them went to the Babies' Hospital, where they were to spend the afternoon. Dorothy, of course, was wearing her uniform and she explained to her instructor, Miss Abbott, that Janet had permission to stay and watch.

The first patient was a little girl of ten whose name was Laura Becket. She was to have open-heart surgery in a couple of days for a congenital heart difficulty, and Dorothy's task was to explain as simply as possible—and without frightening her—what the operation would involve and why it would be necessary for her to have breathing and coughing and shoulder exercises soon after the operation was over.

Laura listened gravely to all that was told her. She was a pretty child, with bright blue eyes in a rather pale face and thick, straight, black hair that was cut short and worn in a bang on her forehead.

"Will it hurt?" she asked once, and Dorothy answered easily, "Oh, you won't feel a thing. You'll be sound asleep when the doctor operates." She paused. "It may hurt a little when you begin to do the exercises with me but you must remember they will help to make you well. Let me show you now what we will do together later."

And, under Miss Abbott's supervision, she taught her young patient how to breathe in different ways and how to cough, and how she was to begin moving her shoulder muscles.

"I'll help you," Dorothy promised. "I'll put my hand on you at the back and hold you tight, so you needn't be afraid of doing yourself any harm. And we'll cough and we'll breathe together—like this—so as to keep your lungs clear. You have to get air into your lungs, you know, to speed up the business of getting well. Now! Let me do a little measuring here, to find out what's the biggest and deepest and longest breath you can draw and that will be my measuring stick"—her round, cheerful face broke into a smile then as she finished—"so you won't be able to fool me and say, 'That's as big a breath as I can take.' I'll know better!"

Laura nodded. She was interested—and trusting. "And that," Miss Abbott told Dorothy later, "is half the battle. That—and this pre-operative instruction to a patient. Laura is old enough to understand it all and she will cooperate when the time comes, I'm sure."

To Janet, the thought of open-heart surgery was both breathtaking and fascinating. She wondered if there would be any possibility of her watching the operation from the balcony in the operating theater, with the nurses and medical students and interns who were permitted there, and she decided to ask Miss Mallory. But this request was refused.

"I'm afraid there wouldn't be room," Miss Mallory told her. "The space for observation is limited and must be reserved for those who have a particular reason for being there." She paused. "You really are interested, aren't you?" she finished.

"Oh, I certainly *am!* I had a marvelous afternoon with Dorothy. I saw quite a few other patients, too, besides Laura. There was a cerebral palsy child who was learning to walk and a boy—Pedro—who was in a cast with a broken back and who was lying in a Foster bed that had to be turned every two hours so he wouldn't develop bed sores.

And there was a girl about thirteen—her name was Annette—who was having posture exercises to correct a spinal curvature. That's all we had time for, but of them all little Laura impressed me the most. She seemed so young to be so understanding—and so brave. I can hardly wait to go back with Dorothy and see her again after her operation."

This was the beginning of Janet's extracurricular activity that she was to carry on through almost the entire first term.

The first party that Janet and Kay gave was a very impromptu affair. It was on Friday night, at the end of the first week, and Janet had said impulsively to Mitsu, after the anatomy class that day, "Come see Kay and me in our apartment tonight. Do you want to?" Mitsu's bright black eyes had gleamed and she had replied in her slightly halting way, "Oh, thank you!" She had hesitated and then added, "I may bring my roommate? She is Tara from India and she speaks English so much better than me. We are in Johnson Hall and we have wonder about these apartments —how you live. It would be agreeable?"

"Yes, of course. Bring Tara, by all means." And Janet gave Mitsu the address.

So Kay and Janet laid in some refreshments for the evening and Janet found places for the last of the things her mother had sent—a carved and polished red wooden box, a round blue vase, a yellow bowl. All of these she put in spaces between the books in the bookcase. She hung an etching of the Chapel at Williston between the two front windows and brightened the blank wall above the big chairs with two flower prints. In the bedrooms, too, were spread the white scatter rugs that Mrs. Moore had packed and that the girls had found in a carton which they had pushed under a bed and forgotten about until today. Now Janet's room, with its pale walls, was a symphony in yellow and white, while Kay's blue accessories struck a nice contrasting note in her room.

At eight o'clock, the bell sounded at the front door and there stood Mitsu and Tara. Mitsu had put on her flowered Japanese kimono, with its wide dark blue sash tied in a huge bow at the back. There were little ornaments stuck in her bound black hair and high-soled sandals on her tiny feet. Tara was wearing a lovely sari of corn-colored silk that had a deep green border around the bottom, and her hair was rolled in a bun at the back of her neck. Both girls were smiling shyly.

"We think perhaps you have an interest to see our native costumes," Mitsu said.

Janet let out a little cry of pleasure. "Oh, come in and let us look! How pretty!" She made both guests turn around and around while she and Kay surveyed them. "But how in the world do you ever get into them? I've always wondered."

So, of course, Mitsu and Tara obligingly demonstrated by dressing Janet and Kay up in their costumes. Janet was too tall for Mitsu's outfit, which barely reached to her ankles, but Kay looked charming in Tara's sari. It was while they had these on and their guests stood in their slips that the doorbell sounded again.

"Who in the world can that be?" Janet exclaimed. "Mitsu—and Tara, go into a bedroom and wait there while I see."

The two foreigners scurried out of sight, giggling, while Janet, in her borrowed kimono, opened the door. There stood David Plunkett and with him a square-set young Englishman with glasses whom Janet remembered seeing in some of her classes.

David's eyes widened as he looked at her and beyond her to Kay.

"Well! What goes on here? A masquerade ball? Or what?"

Janet laughed and opened the door wider. "Come in, Dave, and we'll explain," she said. She held out her hand to the Englishman. "You, too. Come in. I've seen you in classes but I don't know your name."

"Benton. Roger Benton." His eyes met Kay's. "Hello," he said.

"Hello, Roger. Hello, Dave. How come you're not typing for your doctor tonight?" Kay asked.

"I'm ahead of him. He's got to write some more chapters before I can work again."

After the two young men had entered and the door was closed, Janet told them about the costumes. "So now, if you'll excuse us both for a minute," she finished, "we'll give back our borrowed clothes to their rightful owners and get into our own things. We'll all be with you again in no time flat. Meanwhile, make yourselves at home."

"Will do," Dave said, dropping into one of the big chairs. "It's easy. Nice setup you've got here," he called after his hostesses.

He was still singing praises of the little apartment three hours later. By then he had examined and approved of everything in the living room, had turned on the radio, had danced with each of the four girls in turn, had peered into the two bedrooms, and made himself at home in the kitchen, where he helped open bottles of cokes and jars of cheese, had opened up the bread and distributed plates and glasses and generally proved himself extremely useful.

"You certainly know your way around a refrigerator," Kay observed, as he brought out olives and pickles and held them up inquiringly. "All right. We'll have those, too."

It was a gay and informal time, with much talk and much laughter. Mitsu and Tara in their colorful costumes, extravagantly admired by both boys, gradually lost their shyness. Indeed, who could be shy with Dave around? He was so completely at home and at ease that stiffness was impossible. And how he could eat! A three-decker sandwich piled high with everything he could think to put in it vanished in no time and he was ready for another.

"You know," he said finally, looking at Roger and nodding his head, "I like this restaurant. What say we come here again?"

"Righto," Roger agreed. "Jolly good idea."

"It ees so cheap for you, too," Mitsu murmured, her black eyes dancing. "Is eet not so?" She glanced at her watch and rose as she spoke, for she felt she should be starting for home.

David put back his blond head and roared with laughter. "Now who would have expected that jab from gentle little Mitsu!" he said.

"I am what you call fresh, perhaps?"

David smiled at her. "Well—let's not call it that. Let's

just call it smart. But how in the world did you know I liked free meals?"

"I hear you say one time in the hall—it was when Roger wanted to telephone and he ask you for some exchange— that you say you never have two neekles in your pocket to push together."

"Rub together," David corrected, laughing again. "Well, fresh or smart, you're right. But just for knowing so much, I'm going to take you back to Johnson Hall, Mitsu—you and Tara. It's time. Okay, Rodge?"

Roger nodded in agreement, and Tara now stood up, too.

"Yes, it ees time," Mitsu said. "It has become very late." She walked over to Janet and Kay and held out a hand to each. "I do not like the good-by at all. It has been so vairy much fun!"

"Yes, we do thank you so much," Tara said in her perfect English. "It's been a delightful evening." She turned to Roger. "And such fun meeting you and finding we have mutual acquaintances in England where I went to school." She spoke to Kay and Janet once more. "And I do envy you your apartment where you can entertain like this."

"It's been fun for us, too," Janet assured her. "Good night, Mitsu. Good night, Tara. And Dave. And Roger. Let's do it some more, shall we?"

"And soon!" Kay added enthusiastically.

7

A Double Date

THE DAYS SLIPPED BY—and all of them were full. The schedules of Janet and Kay were just alike so they departed from their apartment together each morning, with their books and their notebooks, and caught a bus to Medical Center, ten blocks south. Sometimes, if there was time and the weather was nice, they walked. There were classes from nine o'clock until noon. A break for lunch in the cafeteria followed, then more classes in the afternoon. On two days each week, Janet had her tour with Dorothy Drake. Finally, the two friends headed for home, to shop on the way, to cook what they had bought, to eat, to clean up after eating, and to study.

By this time, Janet knew who all ten of the Certificate students were. Aside from herself and Kay, Mitsu and Tara and Dave and Roger Benton, there were four others who lived off campus, in rented rooms. Two were older women. One was the Greek young man she had seen at the opening luncheon and the fourth was a Philippine girl. All their schedules were different from hers, arranged for them to fit into the various jobs they had undertaken, so she did not see them much. The other twenty or thirty therapy students were undergraduates, Juniors and Seniors, taking the degree course. Most of them lived on campus and hobnobbed together in various undergraduate activities, so she did not see much of them, either.

But it did not matter. Janet was busy and she was happy and she was learning what an intricate and marvelous machine the human body is and how interrelated all its parts are, so that, if one got out of order, others would, too, until the whole mechanism could be seriously and adversely affected. And that was where she was going to come in—helping to set things right, helping to restore the balance. This became more and more clear to her as she accompanied Dorothy Drake, especially after her visit to little Laura Becket.

The very day after the child's operation, Janet went to her bedside with Dorothy and Miss Abbott and watched them help the child to a sitting position. Then, with Miss Abbott's hand held firmly over the incisional area, Laura bravely attempted coughing, to prevent the collection of mucous in the bronchii. It hurt her—and her blue eyes filled with tears at the pain—but, with gentle encouragement from Dorothy and her instructor, she tried again. This time, at a nod from Miss Abbott, Dorothy made a game of it. First, she held a facial tissue before Laura's face and told her to see if she could "make it fly" with her expelled breath. Next, she produced a balloon for the little girl to blow up. Finally, she gave her a "fairy wand," which she was to wave in imitation of Miss Abbott's motions. This last game, of course, was for the exercise of shoulder muscles. All these tricks to coax Laura to do the things it was necessary for her to do Janet found most interesting.

Pedro came next—the boy with the broken back. He was still strapped in the Foster bed and restless and unhappy because he had nothing to read. Discovering this, Janet got him to tell her what kinds of books interested him and straightway she went to the library on the twentieth floor, where she took out a card for him. Selecting several books, she carried them back to him. They were all scientific.

"Oh, gee! Thanks!" he exclaimed in happy surprise when she appeared with them. "That's swell! The library cart woman comes around about once a week—there are so very many patients for her to serve— She seldom has anything I want, so this is really great. Thanks a lot."

"You're welcome," Janet said, glad she could do a little something for him, even though it was not the helpful massage that Dorothy offered, which was keeping his inert body in good condition by toning up his muscles and stimulating circulation.

In reply to Janet's question about his progress Dorothy said, "Oh, Pedro will be in that bed for weeks. It's a long process to heal a broken back. But he has resigned himself to it and your getting him those books today was an inspiration. With his reading rack and his ability to use his arms to turn pages, he'll be fine."

So there were Laura and Pedro, and also the young girl —Annette—with the spinal curvature, who wanted someone to talk to while she exercised and Janet made a good listener. Later on, there was the frail little woman, Miss Meek, whose joints were so stiff with arthritis that she couldn't brush her hair, so Janet did it for her while she sat with her arm immersed in a whirlpool bath. Finally, there was Big Jim, the Negro with the crushed foot who loved music and to whom Janet brought a harmonica when she found out he could play one. All of these became—in a way—Janet's patients, too.

Janet was in the anatomy class and the instructor was saying, "For purposes of study, the skeleton is divided into two parts. One—the axial skeleton, which forms the framework for the trunk and head and consists of the bones of the vertebral column, thorax, and skull. And—two—the appendicular skeleton, which forms the framework for the limbs and consists of the bones of the upper and lower extremities, including those of the pelvic and shoulder girdles. Now if you will just study this anterior view of the skeleton of the head and trunk, which hangs against the wall before you, you will see how this framework gives support for the softer structures and how it gives attachment to the muscles which make locomotion possible."

Janet thought—bones! I've got to learn them all. The long bones, the short bones, the flat bones, and the irregular bones. I've got to learn about the twenty-four vertebrae of the spinal column and the bones of the skull and the upper and lower extremities. And then I've got to learn how they are all fastened together and how the muscles are attached to each one and how movements are made by the muscles. And it's the movement that's important to me as a physical therapist because I'll be teaching movements in exercise and I mustn't ever give an exercise that would pull the wrong muscles. That's why I've got to understand this stuff from start to finish.

Physiology came after anatomy, in the afternoon. Physiology was a little more difficult, Janet thought. Right now, they had finished the chapter on blood and its cellular composition and its six specific functions, and the next chapter was on the heart and the cardiac nerves.

The word *heart* reminded her of Laura Becket and how wonderfully well she was getting along. It was only two or three weeks since she had had the open-heart surgery and the last time Janet had visited her she saw a child no longer pale but pink-cheeked, moving about easily and showing a restless eagerness to go home. It was a miracle, she thought. The heart surgery was a miracle in itself, but Physical Therapy had had an important part in the final successful results.

Her mind veered now to Kay, and Janet told herself how lucky she was to have such a roommate. She was fun to be with—during their free time. She did her share of taking care of things in the apartment. And she was a good student and serious about her work—although she pretended sometimes to take it very lightly and to be more interested in matrimony. Janet, herself, with matrimony crossed off, had plunged into all her studies with an eager determination.

She was seeing now how all the sciences tied up together. Take Medicine and Surgery. You had to know your anatomy and your physiology and your kinesiology for that. You really did. She probably enjoyed the course in Medicine and Surgery as much as anything she was taking, she told herself now. The repair of wounds was fascinating. And as for the repair of fractures— Well! What she had learned about fractures was terribly interesting because broken bones were such everyday occurrences and knowing about reduction and immobilization was so practical if, by chance, she should ever have to use them. More than one evening, she and Kay had tried putting on each other the different kinds of splints for an arm break or a leg break.

But it was the weekly trip to the Institute for the Crippled and Disabled that gave Janet her best opportunity for practice work. Down there, they went into the small rooms where there were beds and, with an instructor's eyes on them, applied their knowledge of muscle movement. The instructor would have one of them simulate an injury. Then, as the student lay stretched out on the bed, she would explain the extent of the injury and the limitations it had imposed on movement. After that, she would demonstrate on the student just what exercises were needed to bring about an improved condition and a wider range of motion. All kinds of injuries and illnesses were acted out, with each student having a chance to suggest—and practice—remedial exercise.

Exercise! Exercise! It seemed to be the most important thing of all. Yet Janet knew that there were other helps for the disabled and she was learning these things, too. Massage was one—and this they practiced on each other also. All the different kinds—stroking, kneading, friction, and percussion. They learned what rhythm and speed to use. Fifteen to twenty strokes per minute for a sedative massage and thirty or more strokes per minute for a stimulating massage. They learned what lubricants they should use in this work—mineral oil, peanut oil, cocoa butter, or talcum. And, finally, they learned that the most effective massage was after the application of heat.

And next term Janet would study and learn still more, she thought. Next term she would have Electrotherapy, for example, and thermo- and hydrotherapy. Oh! There was so *much* to learn! So *much!* And it was all wonderful and interesting and exciting.

One day when Janet was in her anatomy class, a strange thing happened. She had just written the following: "It is known that our bodies have to some degree the power to repair themselves. This power lies in the peripheral nerves which are located outside the spinal cord. When an accident occurs which involves the cutting or injuring of a peripheral nerve, it has been established that this nerve will gradually grow together again, if the damage is not too severe. During this process, the muscles which the nerve controls may be stimulated and exercised by physical therapy. In other words, physical therapy helps keep these muscles alive until the nerve takes over again."

Janet was thinking how very interesting this was when, suddenly, all that she was hearing and taking down in her notebook vanished from her mind as she thought of Dick Forsythe. She did not know why she thought of him now, but there he was. She could see him clearly as he had appeared to her that night at the country club in Oakwood. The strong oblong of his face with his mouth so firm. His eyes dark and demanding—

Demanding? Or asking?

It occurred to her then, for the first time, that Dick had not been demanding, as she had thought. He had been asking—begging, in fact—that she meet him halfway and talk over their quarrel. And she had refused—summarily!

Had she been fair? The thought that she hadn't been troubled her.

She stirred in her chair and brought herself back to the lecture. But she had lost the thread. Well, she would have to pick it up from Kay's notes later. She sat there writing nothing, only thinking—and abruptly she wanted to go home for a weekend. Maybe Dick would be there at his sister's. If so, maybe she would have a chance to let him know she felt she hadn't been right to cut him off as she had that night. Or, if he weren't there, maybe she would at least see Molly and would hear something from her about him. Yes, she would go home. She would take a bus and go this very weekend.

When she told Kay of her plan, her friend said, "Fine! I'll call up a girl I know from college who's married now and living on Long Island. I've been meaning to do just that and, if you're going home, this would be a good time. Before I left home, she wrote that she wanted me to visit her when I came East. Perhaps she'll ask me out to see her while you're away."

Janet promised, "I'll take you home with me some other time. I want you to meet my family. But this time I have a sort of date."

This wasn't literally true. It was much more a hope than a date—and it proved to be a forlorn one. Dick was not there. Or if he was, she did not see him or hear anything about him. She didn't see Molly, either, so she returned to her apartment with a feeling of deep frustration.

She let herself into their little living room after picking up the mail from the mailbox downstairs. It was after nine o'clock Sunday evening. Kay obviously wasn't back yet or she would have taken it up. Dropping it all on to the little round table without looking at it, she went into her room, unpacked her overnight bag, and put her things away. Then she wandered out to the kitchen and rummaged in the refrigerator for a snack. With a sandwich in one hand and a glass of milk in the other, she moved to an easy chair in the living room and sank into it, thinking, whoever invented sandwiches—she remembered vaguely that it was an English nobleman named Sandwich—would be a multimillionaire if royalties were paid on all those that were made.

Steps on the stairs, a hoo! hoo! from outside the door, and Kay entered.

"It's blowing up cold," she announced. "Really cold! Did you have a good time?" Without waiting for an answer, she rushed on. "I did. Marty has the sweetest house you ever saw. And a darling baby. And the nicest husband! I was green with envy the whole time."

Janet gestured with her sandwich toward the kitchen. "There's more where this came from."

"No, thanks, I'm not hungry." Kay had deposited her bag on the floor by the door. Now she moved to the chair opposite Janet on the other side of the little table.

"Oh, mail!" she exclaimed, reaching for it. "Anything for me?"

"I don't know. I haven't looked. Mostly ads, I guess. Or bills."

Kay nodded as she riffled through the small pile. "Here's something for you." She tossed an envelope across to Janet, who glanced at it and recognized Scott Murray's handwriting. Scott was trying to make her forget Dick but he wasn't succeeding very well, she thought. "Oh, and here's the one for me I've been looking for! Good!"

Janet was reading Scott's briefly scrawled note when Kay's surprised exclamation interrupted her. "Why! He knows you!"

"Who knows me?"

"Dick! Dick Forsythe! Listen to this. 'Remember me to your roommate, Janet, whom I met last winter when I was visiting my sister, Molly, in Oakwood.' Why didn't you *tell* me you knew him?"

Janet just stared at Kay, her ears ringing. *"Remember me to your roommate, Janet, whom I met last winter—"* Just that. Just that cool little phrase, as if he'd met her casually only once. She could hardly believe it. Yet she had to because that was what he'd said.

"Why didn't you *tell* me!" Kay was repeating, and Janet pulled herself together and answered, "Well, why didn't *you* tell *me*? How do you know him, anyway?"

"We come from the same town in Missouri. I've always known Dick, but I sort of lost track of him when he went to one college and I went to another. Then, when I realized I'd be in New York this winter, I remembered he'd come East, too, and I thought he might be somewhere near here, so I got his address from his mother and wrote him—oh, two or three weeks ago. But this is the first I've heard from him." She stopped, breathless. Then added, "I'm glad he wrote. I like him so much. He's *nice,* isn't he?"

Janet sat looking at Kay with her thoughts whirling. Her first resentment over Dick's brief acknowledgment of knowing her was gone and now she was glad he'd said no more. She didn't want Kay to know how much they had meant to each other. She didn't want to have to explain the whole unhappy situation.

"Isn't he nice?" Kay repeated. "Didn't you think so when you met him?"

Janet found her voice again and answered briefly. "Yes, very nice."

"But such a coincidence," Kay went on. "Imagine my not knowing you knew him all this time! And I just happened to mention your name when I wrote him—just *happened*." She looked at her letter again and then back at Janet. "I asked him if he ever got here to New York and I said, if he did, he must be sure to come and see me. And he says he certainly will." She stopped as a thought struck her. "Jan! Why don't I set a special time and we could have a double date—you with Dave Plunkett and me with Dick? How about it?"

And Janet heard herself saying—as if she were another person, someone far away—"Fine! I think that's a fine idea."

Indeed, what else could she say—if she didn't want to talk?

Kay planned it all and Janet acquiesced to everything in a kind of numbness. But questions were spinning through her head all the time. Did Dick really want to come? If so, was it to see Kay, who was an old friend, or to see her—Janet—again? Or was he just being polite and saying he'd come and then, at the last minute, would he find an excuse or a reason why he couldn't? Most of all, if he did appear, how would he be? How would he act? For he would have a role to play, a role he had set up for himself by barely admitting having known her.

Kay said she thought it would be fun for them all to go to a football game at the stadium that Saturday of their date. Dick wrote that his train would get there in good time for it and he would come straight to the apartment, where they could all meet, but he would not spend the weekend in the city, as Kay had suggested. Instead, he would go out to his sister's in Oakwood for the night and back to Connecticut on Sunday.

Dave said he would get the tickets. "But this has got to be Dutch treat, remember," he told Kay. "I'm no Croesus." And Kay replied that she knew, and she certainly didn't expect him to pay for them all and here was the money for her and Dick and he could collect from Janet himself. Then Dave muttered something about being able to afford one extra ticket at least, although not three. And Kay told him that was up to him. Naturally, she reported all this to Janet, who promptly declared, "Well, he's not going to buy my ticket. He can't afford it. He's just scraping through this year here, even with financial aid." She stuck to this and, although at first Dave demurred and argued with her, she would not give in. In the end, he looked at her, his blue eyes bright as he cocked one sun-bleached eyebrow at her and said, right in front of Kay, "Well, thanks, Jan. You're a girl after my own heart. And you've got it."

Kay looked wise and nodded meaningfully at Janet and mouthed, "Gone! I told you!"

The day came, a sparkling, crisp October day. Kay was

busy all the morning, preparing the two casseroles and the salad she had planned for their supper when they returned to the apartment after the game. And Janet, cleaning and dusting the place, thought, I'm glad Kay likes to cook. I don't know much about it. I've never had a chance. But Kay says she's always helped her mother in the kitchen and she just loves fussing around with food.

One o'clock—and everything ready at last. Kay, very bright-eyed and expectant and pretty, was waiting in one big chair, dressed in her dark red knitted suit. Janet, all in brown, with her tawny hair in soft waves about her face and her eyes not quite hiding her inner turbulence, was turning the knob on the radio from one station to another as she listened for the doorbell to ring. But she wouldn't hear it if music was blasting forth, she thought, so, abruptly, she turned it off, just as footsteps sounded on the stairs outside and Dave's voice was heard saying, "Hi! You must be Dick Forsythe."

They came in together. Janet, speaking to Dave, could not help but be aware at the same time of Dick's warm greeting to Kay. She saw him put out both hands and stand holding Kay's for a long moment as they both exclaimed over their delight in meeting each other again. Then Kay, still clinging to him, said, "And you've met Janet, you wrote me."

"Yes, I have." He was speaking about Janet, for whom he had decided to wait, but whom he must not push to anything until she was quite ready. So thinking, he simply nodded his dark head toward her and spoke pleasantly, courteously, yet distantly. "It's nice seeing you again, Janet. How's Oakwood?"

Janet, hoping desperately that the others did not notice the omission of a handshake and saying to herself—*what else could I expect?*—nodded back and answered equally distantly, "Fine, Dick. How's Molly?"

"Fine, too. I saw her a couple of weeks ago." Then he turned to Kay again and smiled at her and told her he thought the little place they had here was charming. And Kay said she was glad he liked it, they did, too, and Dave broke in on them both to remark that they had better get going, as it was a long way to the stadium and—yes—he had all the tickets and, Janet, where's your coat?

He wants us to be strangers, Janet decided later, seated next to David in the stadium, huddled against the sharp wind in her brown tweed coat. She was glad Kay was on the other side of her and Dick was beyond Kay, at the end, because, that way, she needn't speak to him at all. So she didn't. She devoted herself to the game and to David and obscurely rejoiced that he was as good looking as he was and as nicely attentive to her. But all the time deep within her there was the hurt because Dick had withdrawn so far that she couldn't possibly reach him. . . . Yet that was unreasonable of her, since she had sent him there. She had sent him there and now she wanted to apologize for the way she had done it and there wasn't a chance.

It was fairly easy to put aside her feelings while they were watching football, for it was a close match and the crowds went wild, first one side, then the other, surging to their feet and yelling and waving their colored pennants in the air, only to subside into a tense silence a few moments later. Oh, there was enough excitement so she could forget herself there!

But it was another thing to maintain a bright indiffer-
ence when they were all enclosed in the smallness of the
little apartment. Although Janet continued to give her
whole attention to Dave, she was conscious of Dick almost
every moment—particularly of his voice. No one she had
ever met possessed that caressing quality in his voice that
could make even talking about the weather sound inti-
mate and personal. Yet when he spoke to Janet, which he
seemed to do as little as possible, his voice changed and
lost that warmth. She felt then that, in his eyes, she was
no more than a part of the furniture there—a necessary but
unimportant adjunct.

Once, when this feeling overwhelmed her, she excused
herself and went to her room and closed the door and
stood in front of the mirror of her bureau. She looked at
herself looking back with anger flashing in her eyes and
said aloud, "I don't care. I don't *care!*" Then she went out
again. Dick's dark glance touched her questioningly for
a brief moment but he said nothing. What was he thinking? Had he *guessed* how she felt?

She caught hold of herself after that and pointedly asked
Dick to help her set the table while David was out with
Kay in the kitchen. Oh, yes, she told him then, with complete and cool composure, she was finding her studies very
interesting, thank you, but she would be glad when this
term was over and she could put on her Physical Therapy
uniform and really begin doing clinical work with the
patients. And was his job turning out to be all he had
hoped? *I can be as impersonal as you,* she told herself.

Dave came in just then with one hot casserole and Kay

followed with the other. Then Kay returned to the kitchen for the salad, while Janet plugged in the coffee percolater. In a minute, Dave opened up the snack trays, one for each person, and they all helped themselves to the buffet supper that was spread out on the drop-leaf table, the boys making themselves comfortable in the two big chairs while the girls took the smaller ones that had been brought from the bedrooms.

It was a gay meal. Dave kept it gay, and Janet blessed him for his easy loquacity and his jokes and his stories. With Dave around, there were never any embarrassing silences, with nobody knowing what to say. He turned the radio on, of course, and kept interrupting the meal to dance first with Janet, then with Kay. If Dick wanted to dance with her, Janet thought, she wouldn't refuse. But he didn't ask. He danced once with Kay and that was all.

Presently, the casserole dishes were empty and the salad was gone and it was time for the apple pie that Kay had made yesterday. Smacking his lips over it, Dave said, "There's one thing about this place, Dick, they always give you good eats. By the way, who's the cook?"

"I am," Kay answered, and Janet saw Dick shoot her a surprised and interested look. Yes, and she wants to get married, too, Dick, Janet told him silently. She doesn't care about having a career. She's just the girl for you. Aren't you glad you've found her again?

After they had all finished their dessert, Dave wanted to dance some more, to "work the meal down," he said. But Dick went out to the kitchen with Kay and began to help her clean up. Janet could hear them laughing and talking

out there and she wondered what in the world they were
finding to say to each other. She, herself, was talked out
and had nothing left to say to Dave—nothing at all.

"Ought we to be out there helping, too?" Dave asked,
with his mouth close to Janet's ear as they danced.

"No," she replied. "There isn't room for the four of us."
Then she added, forcing herself to say it, "Besides, I think
they'd rather be alone together."

For she knew surely now that Dick hadn't come for the
chance to see her at all. He had come because he had
wanted to see Kay.

8

❀

The Christmas Holidays

AND NOW THE ROUTINE BEGAN AGAIN. The alarm clock in
the morning. The swift rush to the shower. The rush back
to dress. The snatched cup of coffee and piece of toast for
breakfast. The tossed-together bedclothes. The grab for a
topcoat, a scarf—storm boots if the weather was bad—purse,
and books. And, finally, the dash down the stairs to the
street, headed for a bus.

It was always the same, except the day they went down-
town to the Institute for the Crippled and Disabled. Then
the girls took the subway for the long ride. There seemed
to be more leisure on that day, somehow. Was it because
of the ride? Or because, when they arrived, their instructor
let them take all the time they wanted to ask questions?
Anyway, in addition to the practicing of exercises she did
on the other girls, and the practicing of bandaging and
massage, Janet learned much more.

She learned that the set of steps she saw was to teach the
crippled how to get on and off a bus and how to go up and
down staircases, that the tubs containing hot liquid paraf-

fin were dips for arthritic patients who could immerse their swollen joints for a moment and then, lifting them out, have the warmth sealed in by the paraffin. There was a table, called the De Lorme table, that could exercise all parts of the body—and another traction table that had a heat unit and rollers which gave a massage.

She saw a "hydrocollator," too, where heat pads were kept hot by electricity and, when taken out, were snapped into towel holders so the pads would not burn. She saw an "ultra-sound" machine which provided heat and massage through vibration and she wrote in her notebook: "This can be used on the skin if the skin is oiled. Or it can be used under water without touching the skin." She saw a diathermy—short-wave—machine for heat—and two "whirlpools," in which arms or legs could be immersed for massage and stimulation by means of the agitated water. Of course, she also saw the usual wall pulleys and parallel bars and ramps and stationary bicycles. And all that she saw and learned made more comprehensible her tours of duty with Dorothy Drake.

So the weeks passed and October went out in a hard northeast downpour and November arrived cold and gray, harbinger of winter. On the bad days, Janet and Kay often had their dinner at night, as well as their lunches, in the huge cafeteria on the first floor of Presbyterian. It was easier than having to stop and shop for food in the rain or sleet and then go home and cook a meal themselves.

Besides, it was always interesting to mingle with those who came and went in the big dining hall, for the whole world was there—doctors, nurses, aides, students, visitors, and ambulatory patients. They included people of all nationalities and all colors. Janet never knew who would be sitting at one of the big tables when she carried her tray to it, but it didn't matter. There was always someone who was ready and willing to talk. This was an education in itself, she thought—and wished she could tell that to Dick, to help make him understand one of the values to her of this year. And then she would catch herself and remind herself that Dick was no longer in her life and whether he understood or not did not matter. Thinking of Dick, she would be glad Kay had not noticed anything of the strain that had existed between him and herself that time he had come to see them, for all Kay had said—albeit a trifle un-certainly—was, "Sometimes Dick is a little formal when he doesn't know people well, but he liked you. I'm sure he liked you." She had hesitated for a moment, then had added, "Let's double date again some time, shall we?"

"All right," Janet had replied. "But not right away, Kay. Let's not rush things."

"Oh, you mean you don't want to rush Dave?"

And Janet had nodded and let it go at that. But she could not help but wonder when she would actually see Dick again. It was bound to happen. Perhaps it would be during the holidays, she thought, because he would surely be at his sister's on Christmas Day and Kay was to be with Janet then, too—and, of course, he would want to see her.

Long before this, even before the Columbia game and Dick's visit, Kay had looked up from a letter she had received from her mother and had exclaimed in surprise, "Well, listen to this, will you?"

It seemed that her father had rather suddenly decided to retire and he and her mother were going to take a trip around the world, starting in November. They were going to close the house until their return and did Kay want to spend her Christmas vacation with her married brother in Missouri or her married sister in Tulsa, Oklahoma? Or would she make her own plans?

"Well, am I the poor little orphan Annie!" Kay had exclaimed. "I don't want to go to John's or Kate's, either one. John lives in a tiny apartment and I'd have to sleep on a sofa in the living room the whole time. And why should I go to Kate in Tulsa, where I don't know a soul and neither does she, because she has a job in a lab there and that's all she and her husband do—just work in the lab. No, thank you! I'll make my own plans. I'll write to Marty down on Long Island and see if she'll give me house room for a few days. And maybe I can just stay here the rest of the time."

"Now don't be silly," Janet had said. "Go there for a few days and then come out to Oakwood and visit me for Christmas and the rest of the time. Probably Scott will bring a friend home with him and we can have fun, the four of us. Anyway, even if he doesn't, there are always extra men hanging around at the club dances. How about it?"

"Oh, Jan, I'd love that! Do you really mean it?"

"Of course I mean it. I've been expecting to have you come home with me to meet my family for ages. Christmas will be a good time."

So it had been arranged. And so it was still arranged.

It was good to be home, Janet felt. Good to be lazy in the morning and sleep late—late—late. Good to enjoy a leisurely "brunch," chatting with her pretty mother, who always took time from her various activities to spend with her daughter whenever she was home on vacation. Good to have a quiet evening now and then for talks with her father. Good to have Scott popping in at all times with suggestions for different activities. Good to have a chance to go over her wardrobe and get things cleaned, or to go shopping at the center a few miles away where all the big New York stores had opened up branches.

There was to be a New Year's Eve dance at the club, of course, and for that occasion Janet bought herself a pleated black chiffon evening gown with a gold top. She already had gold slippers and a gold evening bag, so that took care of that. For a less formal occasion—maybe a dinner party or an afternoon tea—she picked out a tailored emerald-green velvet suit dress that made her eyes look green, too, and with which she could wear either her gold or her black accessories.

There was this shopping, but there was also skating at Holly's Pond across town. And skiing on the slopes of the golf links. And a luncheon here. And a bridge party there. And the movies. And a reunion with some of her college classmates. And—not to be forgotten—a visit to the Oakwood Hospital Physical Therapy room, where she saw some of the patients she had known earlier and whose difficulties and progress she understood so much better now than she had before. Especially did she enjoy seeing Rita Wilks and little Dorrie again.

Yes, it was good, all of it. Scott was possessive—but not too possessive, so she did not know whether they were drifting toward a closer and warmer relationship or not.

And she did not want to know. She wanted life held in abeyance for a while, at least until she saw Dick again and could know for sure whether or not he was seriously interested in Kay. Maybe she had only imagined that he was the night of the game. Certainly, since then, Kay hadn't acted as if he were—or as if she were seriously interested in him, either. But Janet had to be sure. Until she was, there seemed to be a curtain of gauze, like a mist, between her and life. So she waited impatiently for Kay's arrival at the Moore home.

"I love your parents," Kay said. "I think they're just marvelous, both of them."

"They love you, too, Kay."

Kay had just come from the guestroom, where she slept, into Janet's room next to it, and both girls were curled up in their pajamas on Janet's bed. Kay began telling her about her visit on Long Island and, as Janet listened, she was thinking that, already, in less than twenty-four hours, Kay had fitted in here like a sister—or like another daughter to Janet's mother and father. She was thinking, too, that, no matter what developed between Kay and Dick— if anything—it must never break up the friendship between Kay and herself. That would be hard to manage, but somehow she must manage it.

"And now give me the scoop about the festivities that you are planning," Kay urged. "You said there'd be a lot going on. I only hope I have the right rags to wear."

"Well," Janet said, "because it's Christmas Eve tonight, this is rather a home night for everyone. We always trim the tree here at this time and do up the presents and generally just sit around. Of course, the carolers come to sing—

the Girl Scouts and a group from church, too. We can join them, if you like. It's not snowing and it's going to be a clear night."

"I can't carry a tune to save me," Kay answered, "so let's listen to the carolers, not join them—unless you particularly want to do so. Go on. After tonight—what?"

"Well, tomorrow's Christmas, of course. We go to church in the morning. After that—" She stopped as Kay broke in.

"After that—after our dinner, which I suppose we'll have here"—

"No, Kay, we're going out for our turkey. Mother couldn't get any help and she didn't want to spend the day in the kitchen."

"I see. Well, after that we're to go to Molly Evans' house — But, of course, you know about that. Molly must have telephoned you."

Janet shook her head.

"She didn't?" Kay sounded surprised. "Well, she will, I'm sure, because Dick wrote me about the plan. He said he'd be there at his sister's tonight and tomorrow and she would invite us both there for the afternoon and an early meal before he has to go back to Connecticut. I haven't seen Molly in years. I'm not sure I'd know her. She has two children, Dick says. . . . But maybe you have made other plans by now."

Janet wondered why Molly hadn't telephoned her. Had Dick told her not to? Had he wanted to invite only Kay— but she knew he wouldn't be that rude, nor would his sister! She started to say the time was free when the telephone on the table beside her bed rang.

She answered it. "Yes?" she queried. . . . "Oh, Molly

Evans! How are you? —You have? I must have been out, then. I'm sorry you've had so much trouble trying to get me. What? . . . Yes, she's here. Do you want to speak to her? . . . Oh, I see. You've already told her. Well, thank you. Yes, we'd like to come. . . . About four o'clock, you say? All right. We'll see you. Oh, and do say hello to Dick for me."

She put the receiver down, her heart hammering madly. *Do say hello to Dick for me.* Maybe this was the beginning. Maybe it was a little opening wedge—a crack in the ice that had formed between them. And if it was—maybe— somehow—she'd be able to say to him that she realized she hadn't been fair that September night at the country club. It was what she had wanted to say before this but she hadn't had a chance. He had frozen her up too completely the night of the game in New York. But maybe, if she could get that said this time— Oh, who knew? Kay or no Kay, who *knew?* Or was she completely crazy?

Now is the time, Janet thought. *Now!*

She was sitting on the davenport in front of the leaping fire in Molly's stone fireplace. In the far corner stood the gaily-decorated tree, with the children's presents, long since opened, scattered on the floor around it and all about the room. Brent Evans, Molly's husband, was squatting near the tree, hovering over the erector set which his six-year-old son was struggling to put together. The light from a nearby lamp gleamed on his balding sandy head and Janet could hear his grunt as he finally lowered his bulk to the floor beside young Bob, the better to help him. In the wing chair opposite her sat Dick, with Kitty on his

knees, her head resting against his shoulder. He was reading aloud to her from a book he had brought her and her
happy smile—showing two teeth missing—and dancing eyes
reflected the delight that hearing the story and being snug-
gled up to him was giving her. Kay—as usual—was out in
the kitchen, helping Molly clear up after their meal.

But how can I interrupt the reading, Janet asked herself. And if I do, Brent will hear. So she sat in silence and
let her mind go back over the day.

There had been their own tree at home that morning,
with her mother and father and Kay and herself trailing
downstairs in their bathrobes and negligees to open their
presents. These included the new camera for her father,
and a pipe for him from Janet, and a book from Kay that
Janet had told her he wanted. For her mother, there was
an exquisite necklace, with bracelet and earrings to match,
some perfume from Kay, and a handbag from Janet. Kay
received from the Moore family a scarf, embroidered hand-
kerchiefs, and a box of candy, while Janet had been overwhelmed by a lovely short squirrel coat—a surprise gift
from her parents. Kay had brought her some stockings.

Breakfast followed, in a leisurely fashion, after which
they had dressed and gone to church. Mr. Moore had taken
them to a new place for dinner which he had heard was
very good. It fully lived up to its fine reputation. . . . They
had reached home again just in time for the two girls to
go to Molly's.

Janet had driven them both across town in her little
roadster. The Evanses lived in a new development of split-
level and ranch homes. Their house was on the last corner,
just below the country club. It was nearly dark by then

but Dick must have been watching for them, because the front door opened when Janet stopped her car in the driveway and, the next moment, he was coming down the flagstone walk to meet them.

There was warmth in his greeting to Kay, of course and—yes—even some warmth for her, too. At least he wasn't quite so stiff and formal as he had been in New York. He seemed at ease this time, and Janet felt her own tightness relaxing in response. Yet she sensed, for all his change of manner, that he was still withdrawn and was merely giving her the same courtesy he would give a stranger.

However, before Molly's friendliness and Brent's good humor and the exuberance of the two children, it was impossible not to feel welcome and Janet found herself swept into their midst as if nothing had ever gone awry. If Dick had told his sister anything—and surely he must have had to make some explanation at some time—no one would ever know it. She treated Janet as she had always treated her. So did Brent. So did the children. Kitty, with her straight hair in two pony tails and a couple of her upper front teeth missing when she grinned, and Bob, younger and more serious and a small replica of his solid, sandy-haired father—both swooped on her and dragged her to the tree to show her what they had received from Santa Claus. In no time they swooped on Kay, too, drawing her in and accepting her as they always accepted anyone who visited at their home.

Dick stood watching. Janet felt him standing a little aloof and observing the picture before him as if he didn't quite belong in it. Or was it as if she—Janet—didn't belong and he was trying to fit her in again? Or was it Kay he was trying to fit in? Janet didn't know, and she felt confused. Presently, she drew away from the children and began talking to Brent. Dick, then, took her place and he, with Kay and Kitty and Bob, had played one of the new games—darts—until they were breathless. Meanwhile, Brent talked on and on about—what? Something or other! And Molly slipped into the kitchen to get things ready out there.

Soon they were all in the white-paneled dining room, with red candles burning on the gay red and green Christmas cloth that covered the long table. And everyone's head bent as young Bob earnestly asked a blessing. Molly insisted she couldn't help it if Janet and Kay *had* just finished their Christmas dinner, they'd both have to eat another because this was Dick's turkey, that he'd been waiting for all day. Kitty asked her mother to save the wishbone for her and Bob said he'd like a drumstick, please. While Brent was carving the white breast in the thinnest of slices, the way he could, Kay suddenly exclaimed, "Oh, how glad I am I'm not in Missouri right now!" And Dick responded quickly, "Are you? I'm glad, too—very."

Janet and Kay had each brought small gifts for the children and Janet had brought a box of candied fruit and nuts to Molly, but no other presents were exchanged. Janet had received a card from Dick earlier in the week and she supposed Kay had, too. That was all, but it was enough. Presents did not make Christmas. Love made Christmas.

Love! Sitting there on the sofa in her emerald dress, with her hair shining like molten gold in the firelight, Janet's eyes suddenly stung. She blinked and looked at Dick opposite her, reading in that warm, caressing voice of his to Kitty, of whom he was so fond, and a little stab of pain

went through her that it was Kitty and not she, Janet, getting his full attention now. Yes, this was the moment for
her to speak—yet how could she?

Just then, Molly called to Brent from the kitchen to
come help her with the dishwasher, which wasn't working
properly. He heaved himself to his feet and went out there.
And Kitty suddenly slid from Dick's knees and followed
him, calling out to ask if she might have her wishbone yet?
Bobby sat absorbed before his erector set, saying nothing
and hearing nothing.

It was then that Janet gathered her courage. Leaning forward with the firelight clear on her face and a little pulse
hammering in her throat, she said his name.

"Dick."

He looked across at her. Were his dark eyes friendly or
not? She could not tell. His face was in shadow. She went
on, her voice low and hurried, "I've been thinking—remembering—about that night last September, when you
came to find me at the country club—"

A sharp gasp from Bobby on the floor interrupted them
and Dick sprang up. Bobby had pinched his finger in the
erector set and was sitting there with his face screwed up
in pain, trying not to cry. Dick went to him swiftly. "Okay,
Bobby, I'll fix you up all right," he said. Over his shoulder,
he tossed to Janet a reply that he evidently meant to be
reassuring.

"Don't think about it, Janet," he said. "Don't remember
it. I don't. It's better forgotten. It's water over the dam
and better forgotten."

Janet said nothing more. The moment she had wanted
and waited for had come and gone—and would never come

again. Now she knew, without any doubt, at last, that—if he wanted her to forget everything—it must be because of Kay.

It was New Year's Eve and Janet was dancing with Scott Murray at the country club. Kay was there, too, dancing with Scott's roommate from Princeton, Jim Turner, her date for the party because Dick had said he could not get back to Oakwood tonight. Kay was wearing a flame-colored dress and Janet was wearing her new black chiffon with the whirling pleated skirt and the gold top. Above it, her hair shone in waves as golden as her blouse, and her little gold heels clicked lightly on the parquet floor as she danced.

Scott was humming the tune in her ear but she wasn't humming with him. She was silent. Presently, he stopped his humming and she was still silent, as if she hadn't even noticed he wasn't singing any more. He turned his head, then. His eyes searched hers and his hand pressed hers in warm affection.

"What's the matter, Janet?"

"Matter? Nothing. Why?"

"You're so quiet. You've been quiet all evening. And here it is nearly midnight, with everything going to bust loose in a minute. Noise! Balloons! The works! And you don't seem to be excited at all. You're hardly even here. Don't you care about the New Year coming in all fresh and young and beautiful?"

She shook her head. "Not much."

"You mean it doesn't hold any promises for you?"

She shook her head again. "Not many." She corrected herself. "Not any," she said.

Scott held her off at arm's length and studied her face, his expression puzzled. After a minute he drew her close again and said in a low voice, "I bet I know what's the trouble with you, honey. You're still fighting that Cold War."

Janet shook her head a third time. "The Cold War is over," she told him.

Before either of them could say anything more, the midnight hour struck and, instantly, there was pandemonium. Whistles were blown, rattles and little pans were shaken, drums were beaten, and hundreds of balloons, floating down from the ceiling overhead, were batted about in the air until they popped and vanished. Above the tumult, people shouted and shoved and grabbed each other and waved their arms about crazily, while the orchestra went into a perfect frenzy, trying to make itself heard. Through it all Janet stood beside Scott, unsmiling and still. When the noise had subsided a little she turned and spoke to him again.

"Yes, the New Year does hold something for me," she said. "I'd forgotten for a minute."

"What?"

"My work. I can hardly wait to get back to it!"

9

Winter Work

All right, kay. Now explain to me about a cerebral palsy patient and what you, as a Physical Therapist, would do to help him."

It was night, and Kay and Janet had been back in their apartment for over a week. In about two more weeks, mid-term examinations would begin and both girls were spending all their spare time reviewing each other for the ordeal. Janet had thought it best to give up going around with Dorothy Drake on her free afternoons for the time being. However, since little Laura had been discharged, well on the road to recovery, Janet felt as though, at least she had seen one case through to its conclusion.

Kay said now, "A cerebral palsy patient has a condition where parts of the brain that control movement have been damaged and so are unable to work normal control. What I would do would be to help strengthen weak muscles, improve coordination, and teach the patient how to make the best use of whatever skills and strengths he had. The amount of help he would gain would depend on the amount of the brain damage. Now I'll ask you one, Jan. What are the six types of freely movable joints?"

Janet rattled them off. "The gliding, the condyloid, the ball and socket, the hinge, the saddle, and the pivot."

"Give an example of the gliding."

"The vertebrae."

"You pass. Now tell me, what is a tractolater?"

"Ooh, wait a minute! Let me think. Oh, yes, I remember now. I can see it. It's made up of a halter in which the chin of the patient rests as he sits before it—and a pulley. This pulley is operated by a motor that intermittently exerts a pull, followed by a relaxation of the pull. When the pull comes, it puts traction on the vertebrae so the pressure on the injured nerves is released. Now you tell me what a stand-up box table is for."

"Certainly, Professor. It's for a child. If a child is made to stand while he's busy at some activity, he will develop muscle strength just through the bearing of his weight on his feet and that helps him to better head and trunk control. Also, it helps him learn standing balance." Kay gave Janet her elfish grin suddenly and ended, "Aren't we smart!"

"Time will tell," Janet answered, not returning the smile.

"Why so serious?"

"Because, Kay, I want to pass everything and pass everything well. You don't know how much I want it!"

Kay contemplated her for a moment. "I think I do," she answered slowly. "You're making this profession your whole life, aren't you?"

Janet answered quietly, "I expect it to be."

"That's the difference between us. I'm glad to be taking this course—don't think I'm not—but it'll have second place with me if ever love comes my way."

Janet bent her head over her book so Kay couldn't see her face. "Hasn't it come already?" she asked.

Kay laughed. "Who's brought it? Can you name anyone?"

Janet thought, yes, I could name Dick Forsythe, but I don't want to because I couldn't bear to hear it said out loud, if it's true. And I'm afraid it is true, and you're only laughing, Kay, to hide your real feelings. You think I shouldn't know about you and Dick for some reason. Maybe Molly told you how we used to go together and you think I'll be hurt if I know. All right. That's sweet of you, so keep your secret. She said abruptly, "No, I can't. Now let's get on with our review."

It was winter in earnest now, and the January days were filled with cold, biting winds, sleet, and snow. There were times when Janet wished she weren't living in an apartment. She and Kay didn't like eating at the cafeteria every night. Now if she were in Johnson Hall, she wouldn't have to worry about getting food on the way home from classes. It wasn't easy, when you were tired and the wind from the river cut through you, to have to fight your way off the crowded bus and into a shop to buy things and then lug them home with you to cook them after you got there. But once arrived, with the heat pouring up through the radiators and their living room restful and quiet in the lamplight and the brass candlesticks twinkling and the oil painting glowing above the drop-leaf table and her shoes kicked off as she curled up in one of the easy chairs, with Kay in the other, and their meal tastily set out on snack trays before them, Janet wouldn't have it any other way. In Johnson Hall, there would be people all around her all the time and the noise and the food would be pretty much the same week after week. Here there was privacy and there was variety in the meals because Kay was an imaginative cook.

"Peace," Janet said aloud, not realizing she had spoken.

"What?"

"I was just thinking, Kay, it's a little more work living here like this but it's worth while. It's so heavenly when you get here."

"Yes."

"And all ours."

"Yes," Kay said again. "But look, Jan, I think we could plan better than we do, so we'd have to shop only once a week—on Saturdays."

"That's what we've been trying to do, but we always seem to forget something."

"Well, let's plan better. I'll make a list Friday nights, and we'll lay in a bigger supply of canned stuff. Then maybe we'll only have to pick up bread once or twice a week. Okay?"

"Yes." Janet looked across at Kay and spoke the thought that was uppermost in her mind at the moment. "You're wonderful to live with, Kay."

"Same to you."

"I don't know. I don't do my share of the cooking."

"But you're the cleaner-upper, and I just hate to do

that." They smiled at each other and Kay said, "Mutual admiration society. That's fine, only we've work to do. Tell me the difference between a simple fracture and a compound fracture."

"Well, in a simple fracture, there's no connection between the broken bone and the surface of the body. In a compound fracture, there is a connection because a piece of the bone may have been forced out through the skin."

"Good! What's a green-stick fracture?"

"Funny name, isn't it? But that makes it easy to remember. A green stick won't break. It bends. That's what often happens in accidents to children because their bones are not so brittle as the bones of older people. Their bones bend and don't always break."

Kay gave a small sigh. "There's so much to remember! Let's do some bandaging for a change. Show me the pillow splint, will you? By the way, I had a letter from Dick today and he wants us to come up to Connecticut for skiing some weekend after exams are over. I suppose I thought of that now because I imagine I'll break a leg when I ski. I haven't done much of it. Well, what do you say?"

Janet looked at Kay. "You said he wants *us?*" she asked.

"Yes. Certainly *us.* You don't imagine he'd leave you out, do you?"

"No reason why he shouldn't."

Kay's tone was vehement as she answered, "Well, he wouldn't! And he thinks it would be fun if we could get David Plunkett to come along, too. We make a good quartet, he said. So how about it?"

"Count me out, Kay," Janet said quietly.

Kay looked at her in surprise. "What?"

"I said count me out. Take some other girl."

"But—why, Jan? What's the matter?"

"Nothing's the matter. I just don't want to go. That's all."

"But—I've got to give some *reason*. Dick will wonder."

No, he won't, Janet thought. Aloud she said, "Tell him I have a date with Scott Murray."

That could be true enough. Scott had written her only yesterday that, when his exams were over, he was coming up to New York and he and she would paint the town red, beginning at the Biltmore under the clock and moving on from there to dinner and dancing and whatever seemed interesting after that.

Kay nodded. So it was Scott with Janet now. Kay had wondered when she saw them together at Christmastime, at the New Year's Eve dance. But she hated to be the one to tell Dick that Janet wouldn't come skiing. She had a feeling he would mind. She had nothing to base that on, really. Molly hadn't said a word. But Dick hadn't acted natural with Janet from the very first time Kay had seen them together, so she just had this feeling—as if something were going on between them but not going right. It was too bad. Or (she remembered suddenly) it could be Dave with Janet for, from the very beginning, Kay had seen his interest in her. Lucky Janet! With two men to choose from! She stifled a small sigh of envy.

Only three days were left for cramming. . . . Only two now. . . . Only one. That was today—Saturday. Mitsu came that day to ask Janet to help her.

"You remember you say I shall tell you if I need you?"
she had said hesitantly after anatomy class earlier that
week, and Janet had replied, "Yes, of course. I'll be glad.
Come Saturday and spend the day with us."

So Mitsu came. Janet capably took charge and found out
what her difficulty was and where her confusion lay. She
made explanations with patience until she saw Mitsu's
face brighten with understanding and the little Japanese
girl nodded and smiled and said, "You make very good
teacher, I think."

A good teacher. Janet wondered. Was that what she
wanted to do with her professional training when it was
finished? Teach? She hadn't given the matter much thought
because it still seemed a long way off to her. But at Mitsu's
words, she wondered. Recalling all that Dorothy Drake
had told Kay and her at the luncheon for the new students
in the fall, she remembered that many paths were open
to her.

"I don't know," she replied to Mitsu now. "Helping you
has been good practice for me. But—I don't know. What
do you want to do?"

Mitsu blushed. "I like to go in a business—no. How do
you say? An industry clinic and help people there, I think."

"An industrial clinic? Why?" Janet asked. "What makes
you say that?"

Mitsu blushed even more deeply. "Well, I know a friend
and he work there and he think it nice if we work there
together."

From across the room, Kay laughed. " 'Twas ever thus!
You've got the right idea, Mitsu. Me—I'm going into one

of the armed services. Not because I *know* a friend, but because I hope to *find* one."

It was Monday, and the first examination came in the morning—in anatomy. The room was still, except for small stirrings and rustlings and the sound of paper turning and, occasionally, a cough or the shuffling of feet. Janet finished among the earliest. As she left her notebook on the instructor's desk and turned to go out of the room, she glanced at Mitsu. How was she doing? As if Janet had asked the question aloud, Mitsu looked up and gave her such a sudden brilliant smile that her amateur teacher was reassured. Later, they met outside and Mitsu, still smiling and with her black eyes gleaming, said, "They ask *all* that you make me know on Saturday. I am happy."

Kinesiology was scheduled next. Janet scanned the questions quickly. Thigh muscles. Leg muscles. Foot muscles. Apply your knowledge of these muscles to the mechanics of bodily movement. Yes, I can do that, she thought. I can answer everything else here, too. Oh, hurray!

Physiology followed the next day. That could be Kay's waterloo. Would she be able to make an outline of vasomotor control? And vasomotor reflexes? And explain the events of the cardiac cycle? Janet glanced at Kay, who nodded and made the V for Victory sign, and Janet knew then she would be all right.

Neuroanatomy offered such challenges as requests to give the gross divisions of the brain and explain the controls affecting voluntary motion. Janet wrote madly because there was so much to say. Even with her pen flying over the pages, she barely finished the last question—tell all you know about peripheral nerves—before the time was up.

Finally, Medicine and Surgery were the subjects of the examination. There were questions concerning the signs and symptoms of the more common diseases that almost everybody knew about to some extent, anyway, with a discussion required on pulmonary tuberculosis. Not bad, Janet thought, not bad at all. And now the worst was over, for Massage—Nursing Procedures—Orientation—were all that were left and none of these was in the least difficult.

But it was a grueling week and Janet and Kay flopped into their easy chairs when they reached their apartment after the last examination was over and looked at each other out of tired eyes.

"I feel fifty years old," Kay said, and Janet answered unfeelingly, "You look it."

"I could sleep a week," Kay went on.

"So could I."

"How long do you suppose it'll be before we hear whether or not we passed?"

Janet shrugged. "I don't know. A few days, anyway. Maybe a week. They mail our reports to us. Direct to us, not to our families."

A week later, the reports came. They were in the mailbox when the girls returned from shopping. Janet found them and silently handed Kay hers. Then they both carried them upstairs to their apartment before opening them.

Kay got hers open first and let out a cry of joy. "I passed! Everything!"

Janet looked at her and added, "So did I." Her tone was quiet but her eyes were shining and her heart was filled with a deep, triumphant satisfaction. The first hurdle has been met and conquered, she was thinking. Now she could go on. She could go on and finish. And when she had finished she would have something that no one could ever take away from her. She would be able to face the world—Dick or no Dick—because she would have this new skill, this new strength. And she would be busy—busy and helpful.

It was a good thought.

10

The Uniform at Last

It was the beginning of the second term and the first day for Janet to observe clinical work, for which she was to wear her uniform. She and Kay had rented lockers in Medical Center, where they could keep their white dresses fresh and spotless, instead of trying to wear or carry them from the apartment, and she was now putting on one of hers. It fitted her nicely, she thought, as she snapped the skirt together all the way to the bottom, pushed up the short sleeves a little, tucked her notebook and pen in the one big pocket, and then took a last look over her shoulder at the emblem on her left sleeve, which designated her as a P.T., in Columbia University. Suddenly, she felt a surge of happiness because her real work was starting at last, even though in a small way.

"I'm ready, Kay. Are you?"

"Just about. Let's see. We go to the Orthopedic floor in Presbyterian, don't we?"

"Yes, that's where there are patients from the Babies' Hospital. I guess you and I are the only two going there.

We're being divided up—we ten Certificate students—into small groups of twos and threes and sent to different areas. In the end, we get all around, I suppose."

The two friends left the locker room and walked down the long corridor to an elevator. As they stepped into one, Janet pushed the button to make it stop at the fifth floor.

"We're to meet Miss Smith, our instructor, right there," she said, and Kay agreed.

In a few moments, they were at the entrance door on the Orthopedic floor. As they entered, Miss Smith saw them and came forward.

"This is your first day of observation, isn't it? I'm glad to have you here," she said. "Come in and we'll go around together. I'm working on Joe Borotto right now. He is four years old and is a cerebral palsy case, with both legs mildly affected. The treatment is to stretch the heel cords, giving strengthening exercises for the dorsal flexion muscles that lift his feet up. Come watch me for a few moments and then I'll let one of you take over."

The girls followed her to a bed on which little Joe lay. He had bright black eyes out of which he regarded them solemnly.

"Now, Joe," Miss Smith said, "let's do the exercise some more. I want you to show these visitors how far up you can pull your foot. All ready? Right foot this time. St-r-r-etch!" And Joe stretched, his gaze going from Janet to Kay and then back to Miss Smith, in a silent appeal for approval.

She gave it wholeheartedly. "Joe is a good patient," she said. "One of my best. He really tries. Later on, he will do some walking and I'll show you how to correct his gait pattern. But right now, he must do this exercise twenty times to each foot. Miss Ferguson, this is simple, so you may carry on here while I take Miss Moore to another patient."

Janet followed Miss Smith across the room to another bed. There a little girl of five lay. She had short, light hair that spread like small sharp spears on the pillow, fearless green eyes, and a wide grin. Her right leg had been amputated well above the knee but she lay smiling up at them as if nothing were the matter at all.

"Hi!" Janet said, smiling at her warmly. "What's your name?"

"Anna-May Kingsbury," the child replied in an unexpectedly deep, croaking voice. "What's yours?"

"Miss Moore."

Anna-May turned her gaze toward Miss Smith. "Is she going to help me today?"

"No, not today, Anna-May. She's just going to watch me help you. Then, another day, she will know how to help you." She turned to Janet. "You might like to read her chart," she suggested. "You'll find it at the desk."

So Janet returned to the desk by the entrance door and found the chart that told about Anna-May Kingsbury. She had had her right leg removed due to cancer. The stump was now healed, and a Canadian prosthesis had been supplied, on which she was learning to balance with the help of two Lofestrand crutches.

Janet's first feeling of shock passed as she reached for that "emotional maturity" she was supposed to have in this work with which to meet situations like this. She told herself that the child had come through a major operation with her spirit undaunted. Whatever pain she had known was but a faded memory or she wouldn't look and talk as she did. And now she was ready to take up life again in a vital way. Janet felt only admiration and humility as she returned to Anna-May's bed, where Miss Smith was showing the child how to affix her prosthesis. This consisted of an artificial leg and a well-padded bucket seat into which her small stump fitted.

"There you are, Anna-May. All fixed tight and tidy," Miss Smith was saying. "Now here are your two crutches." To Janet she said, "Later on, Anna-May will discard these crutches, first one, then the other. But she has to learn how to balance with them first. There is no tenderness left in her stump, so she is learning fast. I have great hopes for this little patient of mine," she went on, helping Anna-May slide from the bed to the floor and holding her while she adjusted the crutches under her arms. "She has good hip extension—thanks to earlier exercises—and she will make a good walker in time."

Anna-May beamed up at Janet. "And when I do and can go home again, I'm going to go to kindergarten," she said.

"Of course you are," Janet agreed.

She watched and listened as Miss Smith instructed the child.

"Keep your new leg close to your body, Anna-May. That's right. It's easier to balance that way. You know you haven't a foot any more to help you keep your balance, so you have to use the muscles in your hip—the ones you exercised earlier in the pulley. Remember? Now try another step but don't lift all that weight that you've got fastened on to you. Just sort of slide your new foot along the floor at first. It will tire you too much if you lift it all the time. So just slide it along easily. That's good. That's very good."

And Janet, observing, could not imagine a more spirited and determined attack on a difficult problem than this mite of five was showing. She was gay about it, too, laughing if she felt herself wobble so that Miss Smith's hands had to reach out to steady her and lifting a lighted, triumphant face when she succeeded in taking a step smoothly.

"I'm doing pretty good!" she cried joyfully then. "Don't you think so, too, Miss Smith?"

"I do, indeed. But that's enough for now, Anna-May, so back to bed again and off with the new leg till the next time."

Kay, meanwhile, had finished helping Joe with his exercises and had joined in observing Anna-May's progress. Miss Smith, who was called to the telephone then, asked another therapist in the room to correct Joe's walking gait, which Kay and Janet observed until, presently, they moved on to a third patient with Miss Smith again.

This time it was a little girl of four who had a dislocated left hip and who lay with a spreader to hold her legs apart. "Prior to surgery," Miss Smith explained, "I am giving her both passive and active exercises to achieve hip motion. The passive exercises are those in which I work on her and she accepts my ministrations. In the active exercises, she has to do a little work herself. Thus." And she illustrated both kinds for the girls.

Finally, there was a boy of fourteen who had a weakness in his left hand from an early polio illness and who had

had a tendon transplant. Janet and Kay observed the whirl-pool treatment for him, in which his hand was immersed in a tub of agitated water for a certain length of time for massage and heat and to stimulate circulation. After that, he was given exercises to increase his range of motion in wrist expansion and to increase his strength in the grasp of his fingers. These the girls were allowed to superintend, under Miss Smith's watchful eyes.

"This is so I kin git to play baseball agin," he said, smiling at Janet and Kay.

"Are you a lefty?" Janet asked, and, with a shy, crooked grin, he nodded his head.

There was a little time left now for whatever questions the girls might like to ask, and Janet had a number. She was deeply interested in Anna-May, to whom her heart had quite gone out, and wanted to know exactly what had been going on with her since her operation, so Miss Smith, back in a quiet corner by the desk, told her, while Janet and Kay took notes of her words in their notebooks.

"As soon as the stitches were out," she said, "Anna-May was encouraged to move her little stump so the muscles would not adhere to the skin."

"Did she do those lying in bed? I suppose she must have."

"On the contrary. It was a stand-up exercise. I tied a pulley to a chair at the height of her mid-thigh. Then I passed a rope through the pulley and weighted the lower end. The other end was fastened to the thigh band, into which I inserted her stump. Then Anna-May began raising the weight by extending her stump and she kept her balance by holding on to the back of the chair."

Janet was listening intently. "I see," she said. "I think I remember seeing pictures of that pulley arrangement in one of my books."

Miss Smith nodded and continued.

"Next, when the wound was healed, we began shrinking the stump so that it would fit into the bucket. There are two ways of doing this, as I think you have learned, and we did it by bandaging. Gradually, it was reduced to the cone shape you saw today, which fits well in the bucket."

"Did you have to bandage often?" Kay asked.

"Oh, yes. Several times a day. The bandaging not only shaped the stump but the pressure helped to harden and toughen it. You always apply the bandage, you know, so that the end of the stump is the snuggest. And you ease it off as you go up."

"That kind of bandaging we've never had a chance to try," Janet said. "We've learned how it should be done but we've never tried it."

"No, not yet." Miss Smith paused and her glance went out around the room. "I love working in here with the children," she said. "They are often the bravest and most cooperative people we have to help."

"Judging by what I've seen today, I guess I would agree with you," Janet answered. "That gay little Anna-May! Wonderful."

Miss Smith smiled and then she said briskly, "Well, girls, it's five o'clock and the session is over—unless you have more questions."

They shook their heads, expressed their thanks, and started to go. At the door, Janet stopped impulsively and turned and waved to Anna-May, who smiled and waved back at her from her bed halfway down the room.

"I'd like to visit that child every single week and watch her improvement," Janet said to Kay as they went out. "But of course I can't. We'll be here only a couple of times and, after that, when we go to observe anywhere, it'll be in another area entirely. The Neurological Institute, I think. And there won't be any children there at all."

"No," Kay agreed, "the cases will be absolutely different. But that's what makes it all so interesting. Seeing different cases all the time."

"I know," Janet said. "But just the same, I'd like to stay with Anna-May longer. The way I think about things now, I believe I'd like working best with children when I graduate."

"It's a thought," Kay said.

It so happened that Janet went alone to the Neurological Institute two weeks later, as Kay was ill in bed in the hospital with a touch of the flu. She had gone to ski in Connecticut with Dave and Dick—neither Mitsu nor Tara could ski and Kay had not asked anyone else—and had returned with the beginnings of a cold. This had grown progressively worse until Miss Mallory had sent her to a doctor for a checkup. As a result, she had been hospitalized and was now resting in a room in Medical Center with three other patients.

Janet was thinking of her friend as she made her way through the long underground tunnel to the Institute. Kay said she had had a wonderful time over that weekend and she had described in detail the big lodge with its great stone fireplace and furniture made of rough-hewn logs, the long, white, glistening slopes where the three of them had spent Saturday afternoon on their skis, with Dave being especially kind to her because she was more or less a beginner. This had been followed by a good dinner after darkness fell and a song fest and camaraderie about the piano and the blazing fire in the evening. Dave and Dick were both accomplished skiers, and she had just hated to return to work, Kay had finished. "What about you and Scott?" she had asked then.

"Scott and I had a nice time, too," Janet had replied. It was true. Scott had been good-looking, good-natured, and good company, as usual, and they had met under the Biltmore clock, had danced, had enjoyed a good dinner in Greenwich Village, had gone to an off-Broadway show down there, and had danced some more before he left her at her apartment in the early hours of the morning. On Sunday, he had driven her out to Oakwood and they had visited both families and dropped in at the club for Sunday supper, then he had driven her back to New York before taking off for Princeton himself. Yes, it had been very nice and she had been glad not to be alone to think about the three in Connecticut. However, unlike Kay, she had not been sorry when the weekend was over because, somehow, Scott had seemed so very *young* to her.

He still doesn't know what he wants to do with his life and yet he'll be graduating in a few months, she thought now. And it doesn't seem to bother him not to know. Something will turn up, he says, but that's so—so *careless*. Just then she came out at the end of the tunnel and there were the two elevators, with one standing empty, so she walked into it and pushed the button for the eighth floor.

Janet did not know exactly what she would find here in this department. She only knew that the patients would be those who had had diseases of the brain, spinal cord, and peripheral nerves. And she wondered how they would all act—differently, of course, she supposed.

Reaching the door to the treatment room, she hesitated, finding herself unexpectedly reluctant to enter. At that moment, a man's voice behind her spoke in a low tone.

"Constructive compassion is all that is needed here."

Janet turned and looked up at a tall, white-coated doctor.

"Yes," she said, "I know."

He nodded and was about to pass on when he paused a moment longer.

"Some of the men in there have been extremely successful and important in their various lines of business or professions," he said. "They reached the top when they were active. Then the pressure of their work became too much for them. There may have been personal problems involved, too. Anyway, it all became too great a load to carry and—" He snapped his fingers. "But remember, as you watch them fumbling to do the simplest thing, that most of them have clear memories of the power and prestige that once were theirs. Remember that—and help them retain their sense of dignity and personal worth." He looked down at her gravely from his great height, nodded again, and moved on his way.

How had he guessed her slight shrinking? And how had he known just what to say to her, Janet wondered. She had no idea who he was and might never come across him again—as, indeed, she didn't—in this vast, busy complex of buildings, but he had given her now, at the crucial moment, just what she needed—the reminder that her feelings were less important than those whom she would serve. She went resolutely into the room.

The place seemed full to her and very quiet. There were two therapists working with two patients, both of them men. In fact, all those that Janet saw in here were men and most of them no longer young. One was practicing shuffling around with crutches. Another was operating a shoulder pulley by himself. Two more sat on a bench, apparently waiting for assistance or instruction. One of the two being helped was at the wall bars and the other was being shown how to walk with crutches between parallel bars, with the aid of a floor mirror, so that he could watch his own feet and see that he was doing what he was told to do.

There was no one free to explain the cases to her, so Janet simply stood still and observed. She noticed that none of the patients was talking. Perhaps they couldn't. Perhaps the brain damage had interfered with speech. Or perhaps they were too proud to make an attempt at talking that might prove a failure when, clear in their minds, was the remembrance of the way they had once issued crisp orders that had been obeyed. Suddenly it occurred to her that someday her own capable, scholarly father, who headed a fund-raising business, might have something happen to him that would make him like these sick people here. It was hard to imagine but it could happen, she knew, and, at the thought, the last trace of the shrinking that she had felt at the door vanished. She stepped forward and spoke to the therapist who was at the parallel bars.

"Good afternoon. I'm Miss Moore. I'm here to observe. But if I can help in any way—"

The instructor looked up at her and nodded. "Yes, I'll be with you in a moment. Now, Mr. Green, let's do it again. Left leg, left crutch. Right leg, right crutch. Remember? And when I say *one* I mean the left leg comes forward. When I say *two* I mean the right leg comes forward. You can watch yourself in the mirror. Ready? All right. Now, *one—two—*"

Over and over. Over and over. But the patient was persistent until fatigue set in, as evidenced by the perspiration that broke out on his forehead. At that point, he was helped to his wheel chair, which he could manipulate himself and so could take himself back to his room. He went away still without saying a word, nor did Miss Hopkins try to make him talk.

"He's embarrassed," she explained, coming to Janet's side. "He always feels he makes a spectacle of himself and it hurts him, so he retreats into silence. But actually he's quite alert mentally. We want him to get over his self-consciousness." She paused. "We're busy in here, as you can see," she went on. "And we're shorthanded." She indicated the two bald-headed men who were sitting patiently together, waiting for help. "I must start them on their routine. I don't believe you can do anything at the moment but you may like to read the charts on these two. They've both had what is known generally as a stroke, with the resultant loss of motion. They have had electrotherapy and are now here for exercise." She stopped as she saw someone entering the room behind Janet. "Wait. Here's something you can do. Mr. Robbins is arriving. He's one of our younger patients. You can go with him into the Occupational Therapy room beyond. He has come to work on a typewriter, but he sometimes gets a little confused by the group here when he tries to find his way past everyone. He forgets his objective, then, and will become discouraged and leave if someone isn't with him."

Janet waited while Mr. Robbins came up to Miss Hopkins at a hurried, shuffling gait, was introduced, and acknowledged the introduction with a bob of his head and a wide smile.

"Miss Moore will take you," Miss Hopkins said to him. "Straight ahead through this room, Miss Moore, to that wide doorway. You'll find Miss Bell, the Occupational Therapist, there."

Janet had not known the Occupational Therapy room was connected with the Physical Therapy room and thought it an excellent idea. Mr. Robbins followed her now, and Miss Bell, on seeing him, greeted him with warm recognition. In a moment, he was seated before a typewriter, eagerly waiting to try it for finger strengthening and coordination of mind and muscle.

Janet looked around with interest. She saw a man on a chair before a loom, weaving a rug with slow, careful motions. She saw another who was fumblingly picking from a box wooden blocks which he was transferring to another box without dropping any, if he could help it. And still another was attempting to weave a basket. Over all lay a deep quiet and an intense concentration and—what was the word? Determination? Hope? Perhaps both, Janet thought.

She moved over to the loom and stood watching the man

at work there. Presently, he looked up at her and spoke quietly. "I'm learning," he said, and his voice held a note of confidence and a deep satisfaction.

"You're doing very well," Janet answered, and he nodded and repeated, "I'm learning. It's the beginning, isn't it?"

"A new start—yes," Janet agreed, finding herself sharing with him a quickening pride in his accomplishment.

She moved then, back into the Physical Therapy room, and watched while the second therapist, whose name she did not know, helped the last of the two waiting patients get to the wall bars. He was a huge man who towered above her, and she had to half support him in his almost complete helplessness. She seemed much too small to do it but she got him there, got one hand fixed to a bar as high up as he could reach, and then tried to get the other hand up to the same bar. But having to support him so that his body would not swing away from the wall like a broken thing if she let go of him, she was unable to manage the second hand. It was then that Janet stepped forward.

"I think I can help," she said, and took the patient's wrist and lifted it and fixed his hand firmly around the wall bar, so that he was now steady. He did not look at her. He did not acknowledge her presence or her assistance in any way, and Janet reminded herself, leave him his dignity.

She went back to her apartment after her afternoon at the Neurological Institute with two thoughts clear to her.

The first was that one needed insight as well as compassion and patience for this work. One needed to understand the reactions of people to accidents and illnesses. One needed to be able to enter into their minds and hearts.

One needed, in short, to know a great deal about human behavior.

The other thought was something she had read somewhere in one of her books. "The route from bed to wheel chair to crutches to cane to job is not measured in inches but in years and sometimes in lifetimes."

She had not fully realized either important factor in her work until today.

11

Of This and That

IT HAD BEGUN ON NEW YEAR'S EVE, when Janet had been dancing with Scott—this feeling of being different, of being no longer divided. Before that, she had been like a person who both wanted to go forward and at the same time wanted to go back. She had wanted to go forward in her studies, yet she had also wanted to return to the *status quo* she had had with Dick before that fateful evening at college last June, almost a year ago. She had been a pendulum swinging between these two desires.

And then, at Molly's, on Christmas night, Dick had made it clear to her that there was no going back. He was no longer interested. He wanted to forget the old *status quo*. "Don't remember, Janet, I don't. It's better forgotten," he had said. And right then the division within her had ended because a part of her had been chopped down and died. There was only one part remaining—the part that wanted to go on.

She had been left feeling crippled for a while—as that big man had been crippled in Neuro. She had swung like

a broken thing—as he had swung against the wall—clinging with one hand to the only support she had to grasp.
But after midyears, she had got hold of the bar she was
reaching for with both hands. And now she was holding
on firmly. Now she was together again and all of one piece,
no longer going in two opposite directions, but heading
forward. And it was a wonderful feeling!

At the same time, there was in Janet's heart a residue of
bitterness that could overwhelm her now and then—a
belief, too, that she might have, in some way, reconciled
her two desires if— If what? If Dick had been more reasonable. And then she told herself—again—that she was
not being fair to him. It was she who had been unreasonable.

It was Scott who had brought her to face this fact. He
had said to her during that weekend when he and she had
"painted the town red," "Janet, how about you and me
getting engaged?" Without thinking a moment, she had
shaken her head. "Why not?" he had asked. "We get along
all right together. We have fun. And I think you're a swell
person. Why not?"

She had shaken her head again, and he had leaned forward and looked at her sharply and had said, "Don't you
think I'm a swell person, maybe?"

It had come clear to her, then, just how she felt about
Scott, and she had told him, with her usual directness,
"You will be when you've grown up a little bit more."

He had been surprised and somewhat hurt and had demanded to know what she meant, so she had explained,
"You aren't looking at the future the way you should. You
aren't thinking a thing about what you'll do in it. You

don't know—" Then she had stopped abruptly because she sounded so horribly preachy, when who was she, after all, to be talking that way? Had she known what *she* wanted to do when she had graduated?

Like a flash, she had, at that moment, understood Dick's attitude toward her for the first time. To him, she had been like a child reaching out for the bright ornaments on a Christmas tree, as if life were the Christmas tree and the possibilities in it were merely lovely baubles. And he had thought her young (as Scott seemed to be to her), wanting to amuse herself with one of the baubles for a while, so what did it matter which one she picked?

Seeing it all so clearly now, she couldn't blame Dick for thinking that way. It was so true. If she had had any direction at that time—but she hadn't. And he, who had acquired direction and purpose, who had regarded marriage as a direction and purpose enough for any woman, had not understood why she wanted any other. In a way, he had been young, too, she thought, although not so young as she.

But all that was, as he had said, "water over the dam." Only it had left this residue of bitterness in her feeling about him. At least, it had left it in her until that day at the Institute.

That day, watching those crippled men working in silence toward their own betterment, she had thought how handicapped they were by the knowledge of what they had been, in comparison with little Anna-May, who was free of self-consciousness and so could laugh at her efforts and her mistakes. For the first time, it was born in on

Janet how what you become as you go through life can serve as either a help or a hindrance to you.

What you become—what, in other words, you make of the disappointments and hurts that come your way. How you take them. You can fight them, or you can accept them. And if you accept them, you can build yourself, because of them, into someone stronger and finer and more understanding than you had been before.

How was she taking her experience with Dick? Was she going to let it embitter her? But that was foolish! Dick was as he had always been. He hadn't changed. It was she who was changing—and not for the better if she cherished animosity against him. That wouldn't do. It wouldn't do at all. If what you became could be a help or a hindrance later on, then she must alter what she seemed to be becoming. She must root out her resentment of Dick and all her anger against him. She must admit—as, indeed, she had been ready to admit—that she had been hasty in her speech to him last June and again last September. And just because he hadn't heard her out—or hadn't wanted to hear her out at Christmas—was no reason for her to hold that against him. He'd had his reason—Kay. So if her chance had come and gone, then it had come and gone—and that was that. What was left was simply an emptiness—a *clean* emptiness without rancour. Perhaps there would always be an ache in that emptiness but there need no longer be rancour.

All this had gradually come clear to her because of Scott and because, too, of her day at Neuro, when she had seen that what you had made of yourself through life could be something to bolster you in difficult moments—as it had bolstered the man at the loom—or a wall between you and living again, as it had been with Mr. Green at the parallel bars.

She was learning so much through others, she thought. She was humbled in the learning—and—yes—happy in it.

Janet was listening to a lecture in her Orthopedic class and she wrote in her notebook:

"Any physical measure which produces pain, that is, lasting pain that continues for twenty-four hours, must be abandoned or modified. Stretching exercises to relieve on tractions may cause temporary pain, but if they are properly performed, the pain should not last more than an hour and so will not be harmful."

Pain, Janet thought. I am working in a world of pain and I know nothing about it myself. I have never been in real pain. I have never broken any bones or had any serious illness. The only way I can learn about pain is to study about it. She went on writing.

"Pain can be combatted by ice packs, cold compresses, or heat. But some persons cannot tolerate heat and then it is found that heat makes the condition worse."

Like that woman in the ward where I observed last week, Janet remembered. She had arthritis in her shoulder and couldn't stand the hot pack I put on her. I could only give her massage.

"Massage," her instructor was saying, "improves the circulation and, when properly used, it helps relieve muscle spasm and pain. Massage should always be gentle. It should never hurt. You should never dig deep into muscles in an attempt to work out so-called knots. That will only be most likely to result in more pain. Remember that massage alone does not restore function. It is simply an aid to other measures you may use."

Kay, in the seat beside her, pushed over a note to Janet. It said, "Dick wrote me he'd be in New York on some business matter tomorrow and would like to take us both out to dinner. If you'll go, maybe Dave will join us. How about it?"

And Janet wrote back, "No, thanks. Dave has to economize and I have some work to do on that paper that's due right after spring vacation."

She wasn't ready to see Dick again. It was nearly the end of March—and Christmas was a long way behind, but she wasn't ready to see Dick—yet. She wasn't sure enough of herself.

Besides, what was the point?

Spring vacation. Kay went to visit her friend, Marty, on Long Island for most of it, while Janet went home. She had invited Kay to come with her but Kay said she had already accepted Marty's invitation and when her visit there was over, she guessed she'd just come back to the apartment.

"I have a paper to work on, too, you know," she said. "And I haven't begun mine, as you have. Besides—" But there she stopped.

"Besides what?'

"Oh, nothing."

Besides, Janet thought, Dick will probably come to New York again and he can visit with you better here in the apartment if I'm not around. But she did not say what she was thinking. She simply nodded and accepted Kay's excuse for whatever it was worth.

Janet found Oakwood a beauty place. Everything was in bloom. Azaleas, lilacs, wistaria, dogwood, and forsythia made a riot of color over their whole place. Tulips blazed in the garden. Hyacinths filled the air with their fragrance, vying with the perfume of violets and lilies of the valley.

It was a lovely time of year and Janet was glad to get out of the city, where you never really saw spring. She was glad, even though there wasn't much to do in Oakwood because the tennis courts at the club weren't ready yet nor was the pool filled. In addition, everybody she knew was not having vacation at the same time that she was. But it didn't matter. She didn't mind being alone. She was tired and could rest—and she could finish her paper.

Janet had to write about three different patients she had observed whose exercise program differed in its primary goal—to increase the range of motion or to increase coordination and balance or to increase strength. She had to describe the programs for each one and also explain the disease in each case. Since this was the only requirement for all the observation she had done, it was very important. She would work on it the whole week, type it on her father's typewriter, and have it ready to hand in when she went back to college.

She gave her mornings to this project and, in the afternoon, she did whatever came up to do. Twice she went to the hospital, to the Physical Therapy room, and saw Rita again and little Dorrie who was, at last, beginning to walk with the help of braces. She worked in the garden a bit and twice she did the shopping for her mother.

It was on her last Saturday, when she was in the chain store, that she ran into Molly Evans. Molly had both children with her and it was Kitty who spied Janet first and called a greeting down the length of the store. Molly turned and saw Janet, too, and waved. Then she pushed her cart with Bobby in it down the aisle to speak to her.

She said, "Oh, I'm so glad to see you! I was going to call you up because I heard you were home. Dick's coming out this afternoon for the weekend and I'm sure he'd like to see you. Can't you come over while he's here? For dinner tonight? Or brunch tomorrow or something?" And she looked straight at Janet, as if she were trying to tell her what she thought—that this quarrel between them, whatever it was about, had gone on long enough and had best be ended because Dick was unhappy, and she, Molly, who adored her younger brother, couldn't bear to see him that way without trying to do something about it.

But Janet, not understanding the look, answered evenly enough, "I'm sorry, Molly, but I have a paper to finish up, and if I work every minute from now till tomorrow night, I'll just about get it done. Thanks just the same—and remember me to Dick."

Molly looked her disappointment, but Janet's bright smile and swift nod as she turned away gave her no chance to do any urging. It was not until Janet reached home that she thought—why, Dick's *here* this weekend! Not in New York. Yet I'm sure Kay's expecting him.

It was strange and a bit puzzling. But she would have to wait for the explanation till she and Kay were together again.

So Janet did not see Dick—but she did see Scott. He

came over twice when he found out she was home, once to take her to the movies and the second time to sit out on the screened porch with her the last night she was there and play records and just talk.

It was that night that he asked her, "What would you say if I should tell you I'm going into the investment business with my father?"

She looked at him in surprise. Had he really made up his mind at last? There was a half-smile on his face, so she wasn't sure.

"Do you mean it?" she asked.

"Got to get busy somewhere somehow," he said lightly. "Especially with you hounding me all the time."

"Oh, Scott! I never!"

"Well, not exactly hounding but you sure let me know how you felt about my not making any plans." He left the record player and came over and sat down beside her. "It's the natural thing, isn't it? Son goes in with father. He wants me to so—" He gestured. "Well, what do you say?"

"I say—congratulations."

"I don't mean that. I mean do you say yes now to our being engaged?"

She was silent a moment as a vagrant thought came to her mind. Scott would not mind if she wanted to work. He would never say he wanted a wife and not a wage earner because he was easy-going and it would be easier for him to give Janet her way than to oppose her in it. Still—

Finally she asked, "Is it what you want to do, Scott? This investment business—is it really what you *choose?*"

He shrugged. "Looks like a good opening. That's all. I

mean—I don't much care. It might as well be investments as anything else. At least it's a start. So—what do you say?"

Janet knew he was being nonchalant because it was never his way to be serious, even about serious matters. But—just taking the first opportunity without thinking—without knowing himself or what he really wanted from life—did that make him any more grown up than he had been?

She put out a hand and laid it on his for a moment.

"Let's wait and see how it works out," she told him gently. "Let's give it a little time."

"How much time, for instance?"

"At least till I've finished my course, Scott."

He picked up her hand, looked at it for a long moment, then put it back in her lap. "She wouldn't say yes and she wouldn't say no," he remarked, giving her his half-smile again as he quoted from an old song.

Janet felt he was hurt—but it was the best she could do.

12

Increased Tempo

ONCE AGAIN, Janet and Kay were reviewing their studies together, for after the spring vacation there remained only five or six weeks before the final examinations.

"We really have to know as much about muscles as a doctor does," Janet said. "We have to know the location and action of every single one, how they act in relation to other muscles, and the effect each has on the joints."

"Yes, and this term we have to know about the electrical stimulation of muscles, too," Kay said. "Thanks to electrotherapy."

Janet pounced with a question. "Of what value is it?"

"Electrotherapy? Why, it helps to diagnose motor disorders. Sometimes it helps in the treatment of those disorders. But honestly, I'm not sure I'll ever learn how to operate those diagnostic machines properly." Kay sighed.

"Listen to this," Janet said. She read from her notebook. "The qualified Physical Therapist knows the injury. She has been taught the pathology. She has observed the surgical repair. She knows the physiological effects of heat and massage. She knows how carefully to give the electrical stimulation—"

Kay interrupted. "The electrodes must be placed over a specific point and we've got to know the point."

Janet nodded and continued. "She is watchful for signs of fatigue. She has been taught to handle the injured part with great care. And she knows how to reapply bandages and splints."

Kay said, "If we really know all that, we're wonderful!"

"Well, I know a lot of it but I don't feel wonderful."

"What do you feel?"

"Oh, I feel the need of practicing and applying what I know! I feel the need of following a case through from beginning to end! Look, Kay, we've had exactly five opportunities to observe and practice a little under an instructor here in Medical Center—just five. I've been to Neuro once, to Vanderbilt once, to the Orthopedic floor twice, and to the wards once. And that's all. When I wrote up my evaluation of that seminar, I said I thought it should be doubled in time."

"Well, you'll get plenty of chances to practice after finals, because all summer long that's all you do. You go from one hospital to another and practice what you've learned. Every day in the week for weeks and weeks, through June, July, August, and September."

Janet looked at Kay. "I know. And I can hardly wait," she said.

The tempo increased and the spring days rushed by. Where did they go? Why wasn't there more time? Kay said once that she had seen hardly anything of New York since she'd been there.

"Once to the United Nations. Once to a museum. Once to a musical on Broadway," she said. "And that's all I've been to."

Janet looked at her in surprise. "And when did you do all that?"

"Oh, during spring vacation," Kay replied. "Didn't I tell you? The last part of it, when I stayed alone here in the apartment. Dave took me."

"How nice of him. What prompted all that?"

"I don't know. It was his idea. I guess it just suddenly dawned on him that I was a stranger here and should see some of the sights."

Janet nodded her head wisely. "That wasn't all of it. I'll bet you both came back here after each jaunt and you gave him a wonderful meal."

"Well—yes—"

Janet laughed. "They say the way to a man's heart is by way of his stomach. My money is on you, Kay."

Kay asked a trifle wistfully, "Is it?" And then—"You don't mind that I did all those things with Dave?"

"Good gracious! Why in the world should I mind?"

Kay shook her head. Janet could have Scott or she could have Dave—and she didn't seem to want either. "I don't understand you," she said. "But let's get back to business. Tell me for what injuries heat is used."

"Sprains, fractures, tendon injuries, peripheral nerve injuries, shock, arthritis, and sinusitis," Janet answered promptly.

"Good! And now tell me about the four different kinds of heat used."

Janet answered just as promptly, "Radiant or short infrared. Nonluminous or far infrared. Hot-water bottles or packs. And the short-wave diathermy that heats to depth." But she was thinking—that was the weekend Dick was in Oakwood when I was there. No wonder he didn't come in to see Kay. She was dating Dave. I'm glad I didn't go over to Molly's then because I'd just have been second fiddle, which is as bad as being nothing at all.

April ended and May began. The last month—the very last. Janet had thought it would never get here but now she was almost at the end of study; almost at the beginning of practice work. If she could just get through finals as well as she had come through midyears! Then—

Then there would be the hospitals all summer. Three different hospitals to give her a variety of experiences. A general hospital, a veterans' hospital and a babies' hospital. Or maybe she'd be sent to the Hospital for Special Surgery. Or to Dr. Rusk's Center. She didn't much care. It would all be interesting, for there would be dozens of cases and each one different.

She thought back over the observation she had done, here in Presbyterian, and a clear thought came to her about it. She had been most intrigued by what she had seen on the Orthopedic floor, where the children from the Babies' Hospital were brought (little Anna-May!)—and by what she had seen in the Neurological Institute. The two ends of the life span, she thought. Not that everyone in Neuro had been elderly, but many had, and she had observed with compassion the difficulties attendant upon picking up life again after much of it was past and you were left to cope with the balance—handicapped. It had occurred to her, then, that when she had a choice to make in her future work, she would choose either of those two fields—neurological repair after brain damage (which fitted in with her college major in psychology) or babies and children.

"Preferably babies and children, I think," she decided.

By now, Janet had learned how to measure joint motion by means of a goniometer. She had learned how to measure muscle strength electrically. She had learned how to keep records. She knew how to massage and what conditions it was used for and its effects, and how to bandage the different parts of the body and all the various kinds of bandages. She knew how to administer first aid. She knew the principles in the use of heat and its physiological effects and the proper temperatures and uses of the different types of baths for hydrotherapy and *their* effects. She knew all the mechanical devices that were used in exercise and what each was for. She knew all these things. The question was —did she know enough?

There was very little to relieve the monotony of those last weeks. Scott wrote Janet that he was "boning" for his exams, too, and if Dick wrote to Kay at all, she did not mention the fact.

One weekend Janet said impulsively, "Let's go home! We're having a heat wave and it's terribly hot here. Let's go home and get a good night's sleep."

So she telephoned her mother and Mrs. Moore drove in

to get the girls. It was not her first visit. She had come in the fall, soon after they had redecorated their rooms, and had given the place her approval and her blessing. Now she said that it was still charming, but the bedrooms without cross ventilation were, she agreed, uncomfortably warm.

"You ought to have electric fans, both of you," she declared. "I think there's a small one tucked away in our attic. We'll look when we get home. And we'll buy another so you'll each have one. It's something that's always useful, so it's not an extravagance. Anyway, you girls must have your rest or you won't be able to get through your examinations."

The pair looked like wilted flowers, she was thinking. Janet so pale and Kay so big-eyed. With motherly pleasure, she drove them out to the air-conditioned spaciousness of the house in Oakwood, fed them well, and let them be as lazy as they pleased both Saturday and Sunday. They had brought books with them, of course, and did some sutdying, but for the most part they just rested and relaxed. They didn't even go to the club to swim in the pool and, as no one knew they were there and Scott wasn't at home, no one called them up.

Kay telephoned Molly once, saying, "I think I ought to after her hospitality to me last Christmas," but Dick wasn't there and, although Molly invited them over, Kay made their excuses.

"We've so little time and the Moores have been so thoughtful, I just feel we ought to stay here," she said. . . . "Did that suit you, Janet?" she asked, after she had hung up. "I didn't think. Would you have liked to go over?"

But Janet shook her head. "I'm glad not to," she replied.

The weekend did the two a world of good and, at the end of it, Mr. Moore said he had to see the apartment about which he had heard so much, so it was he who drove them back Sunday night, after supper. And it was he who carried the two small electric fans into their bedrooms and plugged them into the floor outlets for them.

"The last touch," he said, as he stood at the door before leaving. "That was all your place needed, just those two fans. Well, good-by, girls. I guess we won't be seeing you again until your exams are over. Good luck! And make us both proud of both of you."

The unseasonable heat wave broke just as final examinations started. Even so, there were tiny beads of perspiration on Janet's upper lip as she worked over the answers to the questions given in all the different subjects she had studied.

In Kinesiology: "Explain the basic principles of therapeutic exercise and give a list of activities which illustrate translatory movement." In Neuroanatomy: "What is multiple neuritis and what are the causes of it?" In Orthopedics: "What are the conditions treated in Orthopedics and what are some of the related problems?" In Electrotherapy: "Give three values for the employment of electrotherapy." In Hydrotherapy: "What are the physical effects of hot and cold water? Give recommended temperatures for all types of baths." In Rehabilitation: "Name the types, application, and care of various supportive apparatus." And in Psychiatry: "Give the symptomatology and treatment of one major and one minor psychosis." These were just a few of the questions Janet had to answer.

With the examinations over, a *post mortem* was held in Janet's and Kay's apartment. Mitsu and Tara came, accompanied by Mitsu's boy friend, who worked in an industrial clinic and whom she shyly presented. A little later, David Plunkett and Roger Benton appeared.

"I warn you, Dave," Kay said to him on arrival, "there are only cold drinks tonight. No food served at all."

He grinned at her and presented a large paper bag he was carrying. It was bulging to the top with assorted packages.

"Rodge and I came prepared with a few snacks," he said.

Kay shook her head at him and went with him to the kitchen, where they could be heard talking together above the clink of plates and glasses and the opening and closing of the refrigerator and the rattle of ice cubes. Presently they reappeared, each carrying a large loaded tray, which they set on the drop-leaf table.

"Buffet style," Kay said. "You can dip your own dips and choose your own drinks. Nobody's going to pass anything to anybody."

They were all at ease with one another, bound together by their common interest as they talked over the examinations. Voices rose and fell above the background of music from the radio. But no one wanted to dance. They wanted only to compare answers and groan or cheer as they compared them and relax with food and drink in congenial company.

Janet looked around the room. Kay was in one of the easy chairs, with Dave perched on the arm of it beside her. Mitsu was in the other, with her boy friend at her feet. Roger and Tara were sitting tailor fashion on the floor beneath a window, absorbed in each other. I am the only one with no one to talk to, thought Janet.

The telephone rang at that moment, and, being free, Janet rose to answer it.

"Hello?"

"Hello. Oh! Is that you, Janet?"

It's Dick. "Yes, do you want to speak to Kay?"

"Not necessarily. You can tell me. I just called up to ask about your finals. How are they? Or how *were* they, I guess I should say, because you've had the last one, haven't you?"

"Yes. They were pretty tough. We're hashing them over together now, the crowd of us. Wait a minute. I'll tell Kay." She turned to the roomful which had fallen silent behind her. "It's for you, Kay. It's Dick."

"It would be," Janet heard Dave mutter as Kay came forward.

Janet handed Kay the receiver, then slipped quietly away to her bedroom.

It was true. She had no one to talk to. But it didn't matter because soon—very soon now—she would have some real work and after that—a job.

13

New Experiences

After going through all classes together for two
terms, Janet and Kay had now reached the parting of the
ways, for Kay had been assigned to do her clinical work at
the Hospital for Special Surgery, while Janet was to remain
at Presbyterian for the general experience she would get
there.

Janet was rather pleased about this. Presbyterian was
familiar to her and she knew some of the cases on which
she would work, because of her own observation through
the spring and also because she had gone around with
Dorothy Drake for awhile.

Her first appearance was to be made on the Orthopedics
floor of Presbyterian Hospital, where she had met Anna–
May, the little girl with the amputated leg who had re-
cently been discharged. Joe Borotto was gone, too, as was
the boy with the weak hand who wanted to play baseball
again—also Annette, whose posture had been corrected.
This time, Janet discovered she was to treat some cerebral
palsied children.

Her instructor, Miss Keane, under whose observant eye Janet was to work, had a few words of explanation to offer before treatment began. She said, "These children are all under six years of age. Normally, they would be active for six or eight hours out of the day. We cannot, of course, reach that norm, but we do our best. We will begin with massage, then muscle training, both passive and active-assistive. Finally, we will teach some balance work and, where possible, walking. Suppose you start with Jennie, Miss Moore. Here is her chart."

Janet read from the chart, nodded her understanding of it and handed it back to Miss Keane. Then she moved to Jennie's bed. She had learned that the child had weak muscles in her hips, knees and feet and could not support the weight of her body. Janet was to massage her first, then give her exercises and, finally, attach braces and help her to balance, then to try walking a little.

She stood for a moment smiling down into a pair of large, black eyes that met hers without any expression whatever.

"Hello, Jennie," she said. "My name is Miss Moore and I'm going to be the one to work with you this morning."

Jennie did not answer. Janet went on talking gently as she drew down the sheet that covered her patient, put her in the right position and, with cocoa butter as a lubricant, began massaging her hips, knees and legs. How pitifully thin they were! How unused! Janet accepted the challenge they offered and rubbed firmly and patiently for as long as she was supposed to. But an equal challenge, it seemed to her, lay in Jennie's total unresponsiveness, for not once did she speak or show any emotion through the whole time

Janet worked on her. But when she finished the prescribed exercises and bent over to attach the braces the child was to wear, Jennie suddenly reached up her hand and slapped Janet sharply in the face, her black eyes holding a smouldering fire.

Janet was startled but she was even more stirred to a quick flurry of fury. However, she did not permit this to show as she caught hold of both of Jennie's hands, held them tight and leaned close to say in a kind but firm tone, "Jennie, that wasn't nice of you. I'm only trying to help you." Then she let go of her patient and finished fastening the braces.

"Now!" she said, and she smiled down at Jennie as though nothing had happened. "Let's see about standing up awhile. Wouldn't you like that? Wouldn't you like to learn to walk, too? Because that's what you're going to do, you know, and I'm going to teach you."

Jennie's black eyes met Janet's, who saw that the fire in them had died and they were once more impenetrable. But still the child said no word. Without either resistance or interest, she did what Janet taught her to do. When the hour was ended and Jennie's braces had been removed and she lay in her bed again and Janet spoke a word of farewell, she gave no indication of having heard.

"Is Jennie deaf? Or mentally retarded?" Janet asked Miss Keane at the end of the morning there.

Miss Keane, who had observed Jennie's behavior and Janet's handling of it, shook her head. "No," she replied, "but she is very unfriendly and we aren't sure why, although we have had conferences about her with our psychiatrist and her pediatrician. She comes from a wealthy family where servants have had the entire care of her. Although she's been showered with gifts, we feel that perhaps these have not been a satisfactory substitute for love and that she has resented being left with servants when she has known her younger brother was taken out with her mother and father. It will be interesting to see how she behaves tomorrow," she finished.

The next day, the slapping was repeated but this time Janet was unsurprised and she felt no anger. Again she took hold of Jennie's hands and again she reprimanded her gently but firmly. "I told you that wasn't a nice thing for you to do, Jennie." She paused a moment, then asked a question. "Were you used to slapping the servants who took care of you at home?"

She waited but Jennie said nothing, although a surprised look came into her eyes. Janet went on. "You slapped them because you knew they weren't allowed to slap you back. Well, I am not a servant. I am not someone you can slap because I am your *friend*. And I am here to help you so that after awhile you won't need servants to take care of you. You will take care of yourself, the way your brother does. I'm sure you'll like that."

The third day, Janet caught the uplifted hand in mid-air before it could strike and, this time, she gave an amused little laugh as she said, "Aren't you a silly little girl! Don't you know yet I love you? Why else would I spend all this time with you to help you?" And she kissed the hands she held before laying them down.

There was still no word from the silent Jennie and her black eyes still stared at Janet and said nothing. But at least they no longer held any blazing animosity and Jennie did not again try to slap Janet.

"I feel that some kind of milestone has been passed," she said to Miss Keane, who nodded.

From then on, Jennie seemed slowly to become a different child. She watched for Janet to appear and she began trying to do her part with the exercises. When it came time for her to put on her braces and begin balancing and walking, she showed an eagerness to help herself that had not been present before. Janet was elated and gave her warm and heartfelt praise and affection. But she did wish Jennie would speak to her.

Finally, it was the last day that Janet was to work with her before going on to practice in another area.

"Jennie," she said that day, "I'm going to have to leave you. I'm going to have to help some other person, but I want you to know that I'll come back and visit you whenever I can, to find out how you're getting along because, you see, we're friends now and I care a lot about you."

She was leaning over Jennie's bed as she said this, helping her take off her braces for the last time, when, suddenly, she felt small arms come up around her neck. She was pulled down to Jennie's pillow and she heard a small, broken whisper.

"I don't *want* you to go 'way! I *like* you! I don't *want* you to go 'way!"

And there below her were Jennie's black eyes, glistening with unshed tears, but, at the same time, she was smiling —yes—smiling up at Janet. It was a puckish smile, as if, in defeat, she still had victory because *she* had known all along

—as Janet hadn't—that she could talk whenever she wanted to do so.

Jennie was one of the cases Janet knew she would never forget.

Janet went from Orthopedics to the Neurological Institute and, somehow, it was as if no time had intervened since her last visit there in the spring. Mr. Green was to be seen walking between parallel bars again, although this time without the help of a mirror. And the man who had worked at the loom in the Occupational Therapy room was there, too, but now he was busy doing exercises by himself at a wall pulley. And—yes—there were once more two bald-headed men sitting patiently on a bench, awaiting their turn for instruction, although Janet was not sure that they were the same two she had seen before. Finally, the instructor was the Miss Hopkins who had been in charge earlier. Janet was to work under her observation.

Miss Hopkins came toward her now.

"Miss Moore? Good morning. Will you stay with Mr. Green at the bars while I start one of these waiting men on his program? Mr. Green is progressing nicely, although," she lowered her voice, "he is very emotional about himself. You'll see." She turned away, saying, "Watch for signs of fatigue."

Janet stepped to the parallel bars and said pleasantly, "Good morning, Mr. Green. I'm Miss Moore. How well you are doing today! I see you don't need the mirror any more. That's fine."

Mr. Green did not look at her or speak to her but he nodded his head before gripping his crutches with both

hands and pushing one foot forward for the next step. Janet
counted slowly for him as Miss Hopkins had been doing.
"One—left foot forward. Two—right foot forward. One—
left. Two—right."

She counted over and over. Presently, she stopped counting. "Try by yourself, Mr. Green," she said.

It was a Herculean effort for him and Janet, watching,
soon saw his arms begin to quiver and drops of perspiration spring out on his forehead.

"That's enough for now," she said then. "I'll bring your
chair to you, so you can rest." As she helped him sink into
it, she saw with concern that tears were running down his
cheeks. He made no effort to push himself back to his own
room. He simply sat there, crying silently.

Janet felt at a complete loss, for she had never encount-
ered anything like this before. Searching for some words
that would be right, she said, "I'm sorry you feel badly. Is
it because it's so hard for you to walk?"

He nodded.

"But you're doing so much better now than the last time
I saw you!" Janet exclaimed. "Now you're walking without
a mirror. And part of the time I didn't have to count for
you. Soon you'll be trying crutches outside of the bars."

He shook his head. "I—can't. I never—I'm ashamed when
—I can't."

"You can't?" Janet was silent a moment, then she said
gently, "Mr. Green, I believe you only *think* you can't.
Remember, it's simply your legs that bother you. And
you're much more than just legs, you know. You're a head,
too. And a heart. And a will. And *they're* all right. There's
nothing the matter with any of *them*. Think how you can

talk. And get yourself back and forth to your own room without help. Not everybody here can do that. You have nothing to be ashamed of. Indeed, you should be proud."

He sat considering her words. Then he took his handkerchief from his pocket and wiped away his tears.

"Thank you," he murmured. "Yes—I forgot. I'm not just legs. I have more— Thank you. I mustn't—forget."

Janet nodded. "You have what it takes," she said clearly. "No matter how long a time, you have what it takes—a head, a heart and a will. Can you get yourself back to your room now?"

"Of course," he replied, looking up at her, and there was dignity in his tone.

Miss Hopkins, who had heard everything that had been said, nodded from across the room. Later, she spoke to Janet, saying, "I think you gave Mr. Green something today. I think you extended his horizon a little and gave him something solid and reassuring on which to build."

"Oh, I hope so!" Janet replied. "For a moment, I didn't know what to say. Then I remembered something I'd read somewhere and I got the idea of emphasizing what he *had*."

"It was good," Miss Hopkins approved. "It was very good."

Days with Mr. Green. Days with Mr. Ropes, the man who had worked at the loom. Days with the big fellow— Mr. Alexander—whose body had swung brokenly from the wall bars that time last spring, until Janet had helped him get hold of them with his other hand. And days with Mr. Robbins who could use a typewriter. Days in which progress was always slow but in which Janet, watching for the tiniest sign of improvement, would pounce on it as an

indication of strength added to the foundation she was trying to help each one build for himself in a new and limited
life.

"I'm not going to count for you today, Mr. Green. You
can walk by yourself. There! You see? I knew you could.
Perhaps next week we'll try crutches alone."

"Stretch your arms on that pulley a little wider, Mr.
Ropes. I think you can. Oh, that's much better!"

"You can't remember what you came in to do today, Mr.
Robbins? Stand still and think a moment. Don't look at
anybody but yourself. Look at your hands and your feet
and then tell me which you want to exercise. Your hands?
Yes, that's right. Well, then, how are you going to exercise
them? On the typewriter, of course. Is it in this room? No?
Then where—you know, do you? That's the way, yes."

Slow—oh, so slow! But you do not—here—measure time
by the clock. You measure it in inches gained, in new words
spoken, in the brief flash of comprehension from a glance
out of Mr. Alexander's eyes.

Janet's next assignment was to the Vanderbilt Clinic,
where there was a treatment room for adults. And here she
saw once more Miss Meak, whose hair she had brushed
while Dorothy Drake superintended the whirlpool bath
for her, weeks and months ago. This time, it was Janet who
tested the temperature for the Hubbard tank into which
Miss Meak's whole body was lowered on a stretcher for the
underwater exercises Janet was to help her do. And it was
Janet who gave her a daily massage that made Miss Meak
murmur, "Oh, my dear! There's *magic* in your hands!
They make me feel so *good.*"

"*There's magic in your hands.*" What a wonderful thing for Miss Meak to say. *There's magic in your hands.* The words made Janet feel very happy. She thought of them whenever she had to do a massage and she had to do many, for she had several arthritic patients.

Then one day she saw again Big Jim, the Negro whose foot had been so badly crushed, the doctors finally had to amputate it, and now he was learning to walk on an artificial foot. Janet was not aware he was in the room that morning, but as she came out of Miss Meak's booth, she heard the small, soft sound of music and, turning, there was Big Jim, sitting on the edge of his bed, blowing lightly on his harmonica.

She went across to him at once.

"Hiya' Miss Moore!" he said to her, his smile flashing. "I still got my harmonica, you see. An', boy, does it make me happy! Dey kin cut off my foot an' I don' care. 'Twasn't a bit of good to me, anyhow, way it was smashed up. Now I'm gittin' me a new foot an' soon I be dancin' outa here to de tune I blow fo' mahse'f. Isn't dat sump'n?"

Janet stood there, her own smile almost as wide as his. "Jim, *you're* 'sump'n'," she replied. "I wish I had more patients like you."

"No use t'git downhearted, Miss Moore, is what I say. What you haven't got, you haven't got. But what you *got*—" and he patted his harmonica, "dat kin make you right happy. An' you give it to me, Miss Moore. I'll nevah fo'git you fo' dat. You give it to me an' it was de fus' t'ing dat raise mah sperrits. Yes'm, de very fus' t'ing. I git dis an' I don' care so much any more 'bout mah ol' foot." He glanced around the room, then added confidingly, "My

music make some others not care so much 'bout dere
troubles, too. I'm never a nuisance wid it. I jes' raise dere
sperrits a little, like I raise my own." And he nodded his
big head reassuringly.

"I'm sure you do, Jim," Janet said.

"You gonna he'p me put on dis yeah contraption today,
Miss Moore?"

"Yes, I'm going to help you," Janet answered. "I'm glad
to help you, Jim. Let's go."

So June passed and a part of July and Janet's practice in
a General Hospital was finished. She had learned a great
deal, as she put the theories she had studied to practical
use, but her greatest gain, she felt, lay in her new understanding of people and "what makes them tick," as she put
it to Kay. People like Jennie. People like Mr. Green. People like Big Jim. And she hated to leave just as she was
beginning to understand them. But it was time for her to
go elsewhere and—no doubt—there was still more for her
to learn in the days that lay ahead.

14

A Discovery

I T WAS AUGUST and Janet had been going daily for two or three weeks to the Veterans' Hospital, down on 23rd Street and First Avenue. She had been glad that David Plunkett was assigned there, too, and went with her for the first time, because the size of the huge place was almost overwhelming as she approached it. She had been a little hesitant, also, at the thought that there would be only men patients there.

To her surprise, she found this was not the case. She had forgotten that women had served in the Armed Forces too, so there were, of course, Wacs and Waves entitled to the same care that the men received, although, naturally, there weren't nearly as many of them.

Janet and Dave worked in the treatment rooms, on the seventh floor in the south wing. Here there were a number of different electrical diagnostic machines which Janet had her first experience in using. She had her first experience in applying electrotherapy, too, and it turned out to be an experience that could have been—but wasn't—disastrous.

It was, instead, only funny. Anyway, it was one she would always remember.

Her patient was a Wac, a Captain, who was there for recurrent back trouble. Janet left her in her little private cubicle, telling her to disrobe, position herself on her stomach and pull the sheet over herself completely when she was ready. Then she could call out and Janet would hear her and would come in to give her the short wave diathermy for a half hour.

Janet was waiting when the call came and went in to Captain Rhoads promptly. But, on drawing down the sheet, she saw that her patient's back was strapped with adhesive tape. She knew the electrodes could not be applied over that. In a little consternation, she explained to the Captain what the problem was and then went to ask her instructor for advice. She was told to get the name of the doctor who was in charge of Captain Rhoads, telephone him and obtain his permission to remove the tape.

It was a routine matter but it took a little time, as it proved difficult to locate the doctor and get the message through to him. Eventually, this was done, however, and permission was granted. Janet went back to the cubicle and stripped off the tape, only to discover that there was a residue of sticky material left on the Captain's skin which must also be removed.

Once more she went to her instructor and was advised to get a can of ether from the supply closet which would easily clean off the surface residue from the tape. "I'll be in to check you in a few moments, when your patient is ready," her instructor added, so, Janet returned to the cubicle with the can in her hand, opened it, poured a little of the ether into her own hand and began rubbing it over the Captain's back. Her back proved to be quite sticky and seemed to require several applications, so Janet was kept busy, rubbing with one hand and holding the can in the other, completely unaware that, as she worked, she had unthinkingly moved her free arm up until she was holding the can almost under her own nose. It was not until she felt herself falling forward over the Captain's body that she realized, with a rush of vague horror, that she was knocking herself almost unconscious with the ether!

The Captain, feeling Janet's weight slump over her, spoke sharply. "Hey! What goes on?"

The words and the tone brought Janet around. She gripped her relaxing fingers about the can, swung it away from her face and straightened up. "Oh, I'm sorry!" she exclaimed. Then she explained what had happened, adding, "I'm all right now."

The Captain laughed and thought it was very amusing but Janet was overcome with embarrassment at her own stupidity and carelessness. She begged the Captain not to let the story get around and promised herself she would tell no one either. But, meeting Dave for lunch in the cafeteria that day, as she usually did, the little incident struck her as funny, too, now that it was over, so she confessed it.

"A fine P.T., you are!" he teased when she had finished her story. And then, suddenly, his face went serious and, not looking at his plate as he fiddled with his fork, he said, "Say, Janet, I want to ask you something."

"Ask away," she replied, looking at him curiously.

"Well, it's about this chap—Dick Forsythe—"

Dick! For weeks Janet had not let herself think about Dick. She had believed she was cured of him but, at the mention of his name, the old familiar pang went through her heart. Yet she asked evenly, "Yes, what about him?"

"Well, he seems an awfully nice fellow. I've seen him only a couple of times. At the game last fall was the first time and then again when I went with Kay to Connecticut to ski. Remember? You didn't go but— Remember?"

"Yes, I remember. Well?"

"Well, I just wondered if there was anything doing between him and Kay? The way he always seems to be calling her up on the phone, I—well, I just wondered. Do you know?"

Janet looked at him and saw his square, tanned, handsome face tense and anxious, almost desperate, and she thought—*you, too.* So why was Kay worrying about finding a husband? She answered gently, "I think there is, Dave, but I don't really know for sure. Kay's never said anything but—"

"Yes, *but*— It's the *but* that worries me." He jabbed his fork at his plate. "She's a swell person, Jan. I really got to know her that weekend in Connecticut, going and coming alone with her and I— Oh, well! She's known Dick a long time, hasn't she? They're friends from way back, so it figures, I suppose." He straightened his shoulders as if he were taking on a burden. "Well, don't tell her I asked you about him, will you? I wouldn't—I mean, I want her to be happy." He hesitated. "But I wish I knew for sure."

"Of course. I understand. But I can't say any more than I have because I'm not sure, either." Janet put out her hand and laid it lightly on Dave's for a moment. He nodded and changed the subject abruptly.

"Have you been down to see the pool here yet? It's quite a place."

"No, but I'm to give instruction there to Lieutenant Ennis tomorrow. She's a Wave and all tied up with arthritis."

He nodded again. "Boy! They have everything in this place for Vets. I never knew anything like it."

When Janet saw the pool the next day she agreed with him. It was very large and the room and the water were well heated. But what struck her most was the ramp that made it possible for a patient to wheel himself right down into the water. In fact, she saw one man take himself directly to the parallel bars (which stood on a platform submerged a few feet) grasp the bars unaided and, holding onto them, hoist himself out of his chair to his feet, still without help. There, standing opposite another patient, he began doing a bending-knee exercise under the eyes of an instructor who was nearby. Janet, herself, found a rack or stretcher for her patient, helped her from her chair onto it and then floated her to the deeper end where, buoyed by the water and without having to work against the force of gravity, it was easier for her to go through her remedial activities.

Janet and Lieutenant Ennis were in the pool almost an hour. During that time, other patients came and went, some using one modality, some another, all under the watchful supervision of a Physical Therapist, a man, and all seeming to show the three Cs necessary for rehabilitation—courage, confidence and competence. It was one more worthwhile experience for Janet to add to her fast-growing list.

It was late Saturday night and Janet and Kay were alone in the apartment. Earlier, Dave and Roger had come in and—as usual—Kay had scrambled together a light meal for all of them. They all had enjoyed it in a leisurely fashion to the music of the radio, intermittently interrupted by their own voices as they compared their work experiences in the different hospitals. Inevitably, their talk drifted to plans for the future because the deadline for a decision was approaching so inexorably.

"I'm going back to England," Roger Benton had said with his clipped British accent. "There's an opening waiting for me in a hospital in London, so that's where I'll be." He paused a moment, then added, "Tara's going there, too."

"Oh, ho!" Dave exclaimed. "I thought she was to return to India, her native land. I guess you've been using your influence, Rodge, old boy, old boy."

"Righto. Why not?" Roger replied, with complete aplomb. "When you find a good thing, hang onto it, I say. And she is good."

"She's charming, Roger," Janet said warmly. "Are congratulations in order?"

"Well, I'll take them, though we've just an understanding, actually. We can't make plans yet. I want her to stay with me in England—live there permanently, I mean, as my wife. But she is still madly sure she must go back to India later on, so we've that muddle to work through, you see. It's a bit of a problem, don't you know."

"Why didn't you bring her with you tonight?" Kay asked. "We'd have been delighted. We might have worked up a real party for her."

"I wanted to bring her," Roger returned. "Only she was going to International House, to an Indian conclave of some sort, and she wouldn't give that up."

"You and Tara," Janet said ruminatingly, "and Mitsu and her boy friend from the industrial clinic. This seems to be a match-making course we're taking." She looked straight at Kay as she finished. "Kay, have you anything to confess?" Make her come out with it, she was thinking, and let poor Dave off the hook.

But Kay shook her head and got up and went to the kitchen on some pretext or other, where, Janet noticed, Dave's eyes followed her with misery in their blue depths although he remained where he was.

That had been more than an hour ago and now the boys had left, the soiled dishes and glasses were rinsed and stacked neatly in the sink for washing Sunday morning— their day of leisure—the remains of the food were put away and both girls were curled up in the two big chairs. They were tired and they were loathe to get up and start for bed.

"I meant to wash my hair tonight," Janet said. "Now it's too late."

"Yes, it would never dry. It's nice about Rodge and Tara, isn't it?"

"Yes." Janet wanted to turn the talk now to Dave, for whom she felt so sorry and who, she thought, should be released from his uncertainty. It was amusing—in a wry way—to have learned that he was in love with Kay, because her roommate had always insisted that Dave was interested

in her—Janet. And he never had been. Why hadn't Kay
known that? To be sure, Dave had, on all occasions, been
most carefully and impartially nice to both of them, so that
his revelation to Janet at lunch that day last week had been
a complete surprise to her. Still—Couldn't Kay sense his
preference for herself? It seemed strange that she hadn't,
especially after he had been so nice to her during spring
vacation, when Janet had been out of town.

But before Janet could say a word of what was in her
mind the telephone rang.

"Who in the world could that be at this hour?" she exclaimed. "It's almost midnight!" Then—"Oh, it's probably
Dave, wanting to say another good night to you, Kay," she
said, determined finally to bring his name up.

Kay threw Janet a startled look. "Why me? Why not
you?"

Janet shook her head as the telephone rang again.
"*Nunh-unh.* Not me. It has never been me, Kay. It's you
and it's time you knew, so go ahead and answer."

With a muttered exclamation—"You're crazy"—Kay
went to the telephone and Janet, with her head back
against the chair, listened to her friend's half of the con-
versation.

"Hello? . . . Oh! Oh, hello, Dick. . . . No, we weren't
asleep. We haven't even gone to bed yet. Where are
you? . . . In Oakwood? You just got there, so that's why
you're calling so late? I see. How's Molly? . . . Good! Did
you have something special on your mind? . . . Oh, you
thought perhaps—what? . . . No, she's here this weekend.
Wait a minute. I'll ask her." And Kay turned from the tele-

phone to address Janet. "Dick wants to know when you're coming home again."

Janet turned her head slowly to meet Kay's eyes.

"He wants to know when *I'm* coming home?" she repeated unbelievingly.

"Yes."

"You mean he wants to know when I'm bringing *you* home again."

"That isn't what he said."

"Well, that's what he meant. Tell him—"

"Oh, you come speak to him yourself!"

"No!" Janet spoke sharply. "Tell him I don't know! Tell him not till I finish my training in September."

"Come tell him yourself," Kay repeated. "Why not? Hold the line, Dick—"

But Janet had risen and, shaking her head violently, had gone out into the hall and through it to her own room. Here she shut the door and leaned against it with her heart hammering.

I don't understand, she was thinking. I don't understand at all. Kay is so—queer. Which one does she want? She can't have them both.

There was a knock on her door and Kay's concerned voice was heard. "Jan? Open up! What's the matter with you?"

Janet turned and opened her door, to see Kay standing there, looking at her, her brown eyes bright with her puzzled alarm.

"Are you all right? What's the matter, for Pete's sake?"

Janet's throat felt stiff but she managed the words. "Which one do you want?"

"What?"

"Which one do you want? Dick? Or Dave?"

"*Dave!* That's twice now you've said— Are you out of your mind?"

"No, David's in love with you, Kay. Not me."

Kay's eyes widened. She gave a little gasp. "In love with *me?*" she whispered. "Oh, no! Oh, *no.*" Then she seized Janet's wrist and held it in a hard grip. "Why do you say that? Why?"

"Because he told me so himself. That's why."

"But I thought— All this time I've thought—"

"I know you did. But you were wrong. It's you, Kay," Janet heard her own voice returning to normal as she finished. "Do you love him?"

Kay nodded silently, her round, bright eyes getting rounder and brighter. "Ever since Connecticut. It began then, Jan . . . and it's been getting worse and worse. I mean more and more. Oh, Jan! Are you sure about this? Are you dead sure?"

Janet answered firmly, "Yes, I'm sure."

She was thinking—I'm glad for Dave. But where does that leave Dick?—when Kay caught her around the neck with a funny little laugh.

"Oh, Jan! We've been at cross purposes—all of us—the whole time! How—how incredible! I thought Dave cared about you and you thought Dick cared about me— Wasn't that why you wouldn't speak to him on the phone just now? You thought he just wanted to talk to me?"

Janet disengaged herself. She still couldn't think clearly. Dave and Kay—and Dick not in that picture at all. It was an amazing discovery!

"Yes," she answered slowly, "that's why."

Kay shook her head as she put her hands on Janet's shoulders and looked deep into her eyes.

"You and Dick—" She shook her head again. "Dick and I are just good friends, as we've always been," she said firmly. "But you and Dick—I've always had a feeling about you two. I've always felt there was an undercurrent of—of something running strong between you. But I didn't know what it was. I thought you didn't like him very much, while he—" She broke off. "I didn't know about his feelings. Only you're not happy, either of you, are you? What's the trouble, Jan?"

Janet sighed. "Oh, it's a long story," she said. "I'll tell you some time but it's a long story and, right now, I'll just say I don't see any wonderful ending to it."

"Why not, Jan?"

"Well, Dick and I simply don't agree on fundamentals. That's why. That's what has been between us. If we—if we meet again—to patch things up— You see, we quarrelled, Kay. Dreadfully. Well, if we meet, he'll just want me to throw away this year, because he hasn't changed. But I have. And I can't throw it away." She shook her head slowly, repeating, "I just can't. It has meant too much to me. I—I've found myself in this work, Kay, and now it's too valuable for me to think of giving it up." She stared away over Kay's head for a minute, remembering the past year. *There's magic in your hands. . . . I don't want you to go away. I like you. . . . An' you gave it to me, Miss Moore. It was de fus' t'ing dat raise mah sperrits. . . . Yes—I forgot. I'm not just legs. Thank you.* She had helped these few and she could help many more.

Suddenly, she kissed Kay warmly. "Be happy, Kay, dear," she said. "I'm happy for you. And don't worry about me. I'll be all right."

But she lay awake a long time that night, thinking about Kay and Dave—and Dick.

So much water had gone under the bridge since she had seen Dick last. So much!

Too much, she thought, with a calm sadness. Too much.

15

Thoughts of the Future

W<small>HEN JANET MET DAVE THE NEXT DAY</small> in the corridor at the Veterans Hospital, near the elevator, she said, "I have good news for you, Dave."

"What is it? There's only one piece of news you could give me that would be good."

"That's it."

"What do you mean?" he demanded, looking at her sharply.

"I mean there's nothing doing between Kay and Dick and there never has been. They're just good friends."

Dave's blue eyes seemed to explode into dazzling bright lights.

"You're telling me I have a chance?"

Janet nodded. "A very good one, I'd say."

Dave whistled and did a little jig in the corridor. Then, as the elevator door opened before them, he blew out a great breath and said in a low voice, so others would not hear, "Tell Kay I'll see her tonight."

He came, but before he appeared, Janet told Kay she

had to write some letters and she went into her room at the far end of the little hall and closed her door tightly.

What Janet really wanted to do was think about her future, which was—suddenly—so imminent, brought closer by Kay and Dave, who were settling their future right this moment. Hers, however, had no direction as yet, although only a week was left for her at the Veterans Hospital before she would be embarking on her last assignment. And after that—what? She didn't know. She hadn't decided. And it had come to her that she hadn't decided because she was more or less involved with Scott and she would have to decide about him before she could decide about anything else.

Scott—she hadn't seen him much this summer, although she could understand why. She hadn't been home very often and, when she had gone, she hadn't always let him know she was there. She had told herself that she was tired and needed the rest and quiet, which she would not have if she telephoned him, for he would have rushed her off to the Club, probably, to play tennis or dance, and she hadn't felt like doing either.

Of course, he could have met her here in the city more than he had, but she could understand about that, too. Scott was unaccustomed to working, to commuting, and to the heat in New York in the summer. Like her, he had found Oakwood a Mecca when his work was done and it was natural that he should have headed for it at the end of his day, for a refreshing swim in the pool and the comfort of informal sport clothes at home. So they had both contented themselves with long talks over the telephone and the promise that they would meet soon. Still—

Still what? Sitting there at her desk, staring at nothing, Janet asked herself some straightforward questions. Why hadn't they seen more of each other than they had? Was Scott so spoiled that he had considered only his own comfort through the weeks? But no more than she was, because she had considered only *her* own comfort, too. No, there was more to it than that.

She did not like facing the next question, for it was not flattering, but this was a time for honesty, not flattery.

Was Scott, perhaps—with her as with the job he had taken in his father's office—simply following the line of least resistance? Was it because he had always known her, was used to her, and she was *there* that he had thought of marrying her? Hadn't it seemed—well—the easiest thing for him to do?

She recalled his words to her, so casually put. "Janet, how about you and me getting engaged? We get along all right together. We have fun. So why not?" And again, when she had told him she would let him know her answer after she had finished her training, he had said, with a half-smile, "She wouldn't say Yes and she wouldn't say No." At the time, she had felt she had hurt him, but she thought now that it was only his pride she had hurt, for how much *caring* lay behind that casualness and that half-smile? Was it really love like the love she had seen explode in David's eyes when he spoke of Kay? And like the love she had seen lighting up Kay's face when she talked of David?

Janet sat very quiet, still staring at nothing but seeing something clearly, just the same. She was seeing Kay's tremulous excitement and happiness again and she knew that she had no such feeling for Scott—and never had had. But without it—without, too, a compelling desire and need to share everything that life offered, marriage could not possibly be a success. And at that moment a memory flashed into her mind and she could hear Dick saying, "I don't want you if you're not certain about me. It's too big a risk." She understood what he meant now. Oh, how well she understood it!

"I didn't mind one bit not seeing Scott much this summer," she said aloud. "I didn't mind one single bit."

Suddenly, Janet straightened up, reached for a sheet of notepaper in a cubbyhole of her desk and began writing. She wrote swiftly, without any hesitancy or any groping for words, because she knew exactly what she wanted to say.

Dear Scott,

I haven't seen very much of you this summer and perhaps that's my fault as much as yours. Anyway, we've been together so little that I'm not sure whether you are really liking the investment business or not. You always brushed off the questions when I asked you. But I do hope you are. I hope it's as interesting to you as my work is to me because I can't imagine anything more awful than having to do every day something you don't care about doing, something your heart isn't really in.

And that brings me, Scott, to my reason for writing you now. I promised to give you my answer about marrying you when I finished my training. Well, I haven't quite finished it yet but, as I've found out what the answer is, I think it's only fair not to keep you waiting for it any longer.

Scott, my heart isn't in it. It simply isn't in the thought of spending the rest of my life with you and that's the plain and simple truth. I like you a lot. I enjoy our friendship. But that's all I can think of enjoying. I'm sorry if I disappoint you but that's the way it is.

So let's leave it at that, shall we? And just go on enjoying each other as much as we can for as long as we can.

With best wishes to you always,

Sincerely

Janet

She read the letter over carefully, folded it, and put it in an envelope, then sealed, addressed and stamped that.

It was done. It was finished. That much of her future was settled, anyway.

The next week, Janet learned she was assigned for her last hospital experience to the Hospital for Special Surgery, on East River Drive at 70th Street. She knew from Kay's having been there that it was a very expensive Rehabilitation Center and was considered one of the best.

Here Janet found that her patients were of extremely high caliber, coming from all over the United States, as well as many from other countries. There was a large group of paraplegics, also several quadriplegics, with whom she chiefly worked. It was tragic to discover that most of these were young people about her own age who had been injured in automobile accidents and, as a result, would probably be confined to wheel chairs for the rest of their lives. In spite of this, Janet discovered, too, that there was an amazing amount of courage among them all—and it was not a grim courage. It was, rather, quiet and resolute and almost always optimistic, for these handicapped young people had accepted their misfortunes and were building new lives to some kind of usefulness, in spite of their physical limitations.

There was young Ned Oliphant, whose spine had been injured when diving, so that his hopes of ever walking again were almost nil. Yet he was planning to finish his college course, majoring in science, and then to set up a radio shop in his own home.

"It may even be more than just a radio shop," he said to Janet one day. "I may have gifts there, too, to sell at Christmastime—unusual cards and things that can't be found in the department stores. Radios will always be my chief interest, of course—I expect to be a repair man— but there's no reason why I can't have other interests, too, is there?" And his black eyes sparked a challenge as they met hers.

And there was Joe Allen, only twenty-six and the father of two children, who had been in a bad car smash-up. Janet had to give him general conditioning exercises and muscle re-education to those muscles only partially damaged. It was distressing to work with him because he so easily lost the little control he had developed over his own spasticity. Yet he never despaired himself and looked forward to the independence he would have when he could function from a wheel chair at home.

It was this patient who would say with bright cheerfulness, "My wife and I will have to change roles. She'll be the wage earner and I'll be the stay-at-home—the cook. My Dad is very handy with tools and he's fixing our kitchen over, so I'll be able to reach everything myself. I'll be able to cook and clean up without any help. Isn't that wonderful? Of course, I'll have to have help with the kiddies, but we'll work things out with a nursery school somehow."

"People like Ned and Joe Allen make me realize I should never complain about a thing," Janet said to Kay when she was telling her friend about them. "They're inspiring, really, they are." And Kay nodded understandingly.

"At first I was a little depressed, working with such helpless cases," she said to Janet, "but after awhile I found I could relate to them because they were around my age. I never got over counting myself lucky to be—*sound*."

Kay was radiantly happy these days, for she and Dave were planning an early marriage. Kay had already written her parents that she and Dave would fly home, after they finished training, for a small, informal wedding before they had to return to their first jobs.

"Will you come to our wedding, Jan?" she had asked. "I want you, you know."

Janet had replied, "I'll be thinking of you, Kay, and I'll be with you in spirit, but you'll have your sister to stand up with you and you won't need me. Besides, it's an awful rush, so—include me out," she had finished with a warm smile.

Kay, who had seen the faint wistfulness that lay behind Janet's smile, had nodded understandingly. Janet was still thinking of Dick, she had told herself, and it would be difficult for her to take part in a joyful occasion like a wedding when there was none in prospect for her. Oh, she did wish those two could get together again and patch up their differences! Dick's attitude, as given to her by Janet, was simply incomprehensible to her and somehow didn't sound like him at all.

"Besides," Janet had added to Kay, "I've got to decide what I'm going to do—and where—and stick around for interviews."

There were plenty of openings, she knew that, for she had been in touch with the Placement Bureau of the National Association of Physical Therapists, which she had joined. She had found that what Dr. Dearborn had said months ago was true. There were more opportunities than there were therapists. She could go to any one of a number of hospitals all over the country, if she so desired.

She could, for example, go to Pittsburgh, where there was a splendid opening. But why Pittsburgh? Going there, she would, of course, have to take the state examinations, and if there were anything drawing her powerfully to that city, she would take them. But nothing was, so she didn't give Pittsburgh a second thought.

Or she could go out to the Middlewest, to some state where examinations were not required by law. But—again —nothing drew her out there, either.

Kay, of course, was going to stay right in New York City, where both she and Dave had already signed up to go to the same hospital. Mitsu, likewise, was to be in New York, for she, too, would be married in the fall, to her boy friend in the industrial clinic. Tara and Roger were both going to England, as originally planned.

Of course, if Janet wanted to stay in New York, which she was seriously considering doing, she would have to find a place to live, for she and Kay must give up their apartment at the beginning of the new college year, toward the end of September, to make room for other students. With Kay and Mitsu both getting married, Janet would have to find a place for herself alone. And she did not want to do this, either, for living alone was no fun, especially in a place like New York City. Yet there was no one else she knew among the graduates with whom she would care to share living quarters.

"New York is out, too," she said to herself, "and I don't want to go far away, so—"

So why didn't she find out if there would be an opening in Oakwood, where, in a sense, she had started her career? If there were, she could live at home and that suited her perfectly. Once out in the open, the idea, which had lain, unadmitted, below the surface of her mind for a long time, bloomed like a flower. Yes, she would arrange for an interview with Miss Dennis, who engaged all new personnel at the Oakwood hospital, and find out what the situation was there. Of course, she would have to take the New Jersey state examinations but the thought did not trouble her. For one thing, examinations by now were only a routine matter, since she felt well grounded in her profession. Besides, in this instance, Oakwood was her own deliberate choice, so she was willing to go through with whatever might be required in order to get there.

She did not ask herself why it was that Oakwood appealed to her so strongly, for she would not admit to herself that thoughts of seeing Dick again had anything to do with it.

It was the following weekend and Janet was at the hospital in her home town, facing Miss Dennis in her office.

"Certainly I remember you," Miss Dennis said. "You were a volunteer here all last summer and it was your experience with us that made you decide to take up Physical Therapy. Am I right?" When Janet nodded, she went on, "I've kept in touch with your progress through your mother. What have you in mind for the future?"

Janet took the proffered opening and replied instantly, "I'd like to come here, if there's any chance of your needing me."

Miss Dennis smiled. "I was hoping you'd say that," she told Janet, "because there's more than a chance. Rita Wilks is to be married this fall and we'll be shorthanded. If you would really like to join us, I'd be very happy to have you. You will live at home, I suppose?"

"Yes, of course."

"Then let's consider the matter settled. I suppose you'll take the state examinations this October?"

"Yes," Janet said again.

It was as easy as that, Janet thought. She thanked Miss Dennis and, after a few more words, left to make her way up to the Physical Therapy room, to see Rita and little Dorrie. But Dorrie was gone.

"She's home and walking very well with her braces and thrilled over kindergarten," Rita told Janet.

"I'm so glad," Janet said. "I'm so glad for her. And I'm glad for you, too, Rita. Miss Dennis has told me your fine news. Only I'm awfully sorry you're not to be here when I come."

"Are you coming? Really?"

"It won't be long now," Janet replied. "I've only a few

weeks left of my clinical practice. But—as I said—I do wish you were to be here with me."

"But I will be here!" Rita returned. "I'm not going to give up this work entirely. Didn't Miss Dennis explain that? I'm to be here on a part-time basis. That's one of the good things about this profession, Janet. You can work it in with matrimony. I'll have a half day I can give to it and still keep a nice home for my husband."

"Oh," Janet spoke slowly, "I see. That's—that's a wonderful arrangement, isn't it?"

She wasn't really as surprised as she sounded, though, for Kay, too, was working out her career with matrimony— and on a full time schedule, not a part-time one. So was Mitsu. It could be done. All you needed was the cooperation of the man you were going to marry. If she had wanted to marry Scott, she was sure he would have cooperated, if for no other reason than that it would have been easier to agree with her than to oppose her. But she hadn't wanted to marry him, so that was that.

It was Janet's last week of work—and it was an extra busy one, for, besides her daily trips to the Center where, patiently, slowly, cheerfully, she helped the crippled to a degree more of physical comfort, to a degree more of physical independence and to a degree more of spiritual strength, she and Kay had to clear out their apartment and leave it as they had found it a year ago.

Much of what was there Janet had offered to Kay, with her mother's permission. The curtains, for one thing. The stretch slip covers for the easy chairs, the small round table that stood between them, the three white rugs, the two electric fans and a lamp and the pair of brass candle-sticks. Also Janet's own fiesta ware.

"Oh, that's wonderful!" Kay had exclaimed, and Dave had added, "It sure is, because, as Mitsu long ago discovered, I haven't two extra nickels to 'push together' for house furnishings."

Finally, everything was packed and what was to go home again was ready for Tim to collect in his truck. What Kay was to have, she and Dave had already taken to the tiny place they had found for themselves in the Village.

They were both down there this evening, having gone with their last load in a borrowed car, and Janet was alone in the bare-looking living room when the telephone rang.

"Probably Mother," Janet said to herself, "to tell me when to expect Tim tomorrow."

But it was not her mother. It was Dick's voice she heard.

"Janet? Dick speaking. Dick Forsythe."

Dick! Why Dick? When Kay had written him of her engagement? Janet said uncertainly, "Yes—yes—I know—"

He broke in on her abruptly. "Janet, I have some rather bad news to give you. Molly and Brent and the children have all been in an automobile accident."

"What? Oh, no! Oh, Dick, I'm terribly sorry! Is anyone badly hurt?"

"Yes, they're all hurt." She heard his voice hard with his anxiety. "Some more than others. They were on their way home from a weekend in Connecticut when a truck side-swiped their car, just as they reached the outskirts of Oak-wood, and threw it against a stone wall. They're all hurt, Janet, but Kitty is hurt the worst of all."

"Dick—" Janet could scarcely breathe from surprise and

shock and a sudden wave of great pity. Kitty, his favorite. Once he had said to her, "She's just the kind of little girl I'd like to have." "Dick, tell me," she urged.

"Her back is broken, Janet," he said.

She gave a gasp. That could mean so many things—and some so terrible. "Oh, *no!*" she protested. "How badly?"

"That's all I know so far. She's in the Oakwood Hospital and I'm calling from Molly's. She's at the hospital, too, for a dislocated shoulder and a broken arm and two cracked ribs. They're all there. Brent has a bad leg. Knee. And Bobby—Thank goodness, he's only cut and bruised. It's Kitty—" He stopped.

"Dick—" What words were there to say. "Dick, listen. I'm coming. I'll be there soon." Why had she said that? Was that any comfort to him?

"Yes, that's why I called you. I thought you'd want to know."

She said, "Tell Molly not to despair. And don't you, either, Dick, because wonderful things are being done for people nowadays. Miracles, really. Remember that, Dick."

"I will."

"And—and thanks for calling me."

He said again, "I thought you'd want to know."

Was he reaching to her for help? For encouragement? For what? She didn't know. Slowly, she hung up the receiver.

16

A Quarrel Ends

JANET HAD BEEN HOME FOR SEVERAL WEEKS. "Where I belong," she told herself. "Where I'm needed."

It was chiefly Kitty who made her feel that way, for, from the very beginning of her work at the Oakwood Hospital, Kitty had become her special charge. The child had called for her, knowing her, and Molly and Brent had asked that Janet be permitted to be with her as much as possible. So it was Janet who bathed the injured child and massaged her and put her through what conditioning exercises she was permitted as she lay bound in her cast and strapped to her bed. And it was Janet who first changed her tears to smiles and her fear to confidence. Kitty's quick and eager response warmed Janet's heart even more than the gratitude of Molly and Brent, who said, "You're just made for this work, Janet. We feel so much better to know you're here with our little girl."

The final outcome of the accident was still in doubt. In the beginning, X-rays had shown three cracked vertebrae and one that was broken but by October Kitty was still in the Foster bed, which had to be rotated every two hours. This task also was assigned to Janet.

She had other patients, too, of course. Her day's "load" consisted of about ten altogether, counting Kitty. But Kitty was her greatest concern, partly because here was a case that she—Janet—would follow from the beginning to the end—something she had always wanted—partly, also, because the child was showing the wonderful resilience of spirit that children often possessed, but chiefly because Kitty was the daughter of old friends—and Dick's niece.

As for Dick, he drove from Connecticut to Molly's every weekend. And every weekend he brought some unexpected gift to the little invalid when he went to see her. He had become almost as well-known a figure there in the hospital as her father was. Indeed, he often came instead of Brent who, still on crutches, found it difficult to get in and out of his car and so sometimes let Molly and Dick check without him.

Janet knew the visiting hours and so knew when they would call. She would watch for them—for Molly with her arm still in a sling, accompanied by the tall, dark man whose face was so familiar to her. She was not always at Kitty's side when they appeared but she was always aware of them, especially of Dick. She could feel his eyes on her as she moved about the room, doing whatever she had to do. Sometimes he even followed behind her, to chat briefly with those she had been helping. It was a curiosity and interest she had not expected to find in him and she wondered what he was thinking about it all?

Eventually, of course, she would join both of the visitors by Kitty's bed where Molly welcomed her as the one person she felt sure she could rely on to give her truthful answers to the questions she had to ask about her child. Dick, too, had questions—not only concerning Kitty but about Janet's work in general. Then he would stand listening to her answers with a grave and quiet attention.

"This is all a revelation to me," he said once. "I'm glad to learn about it. I had no idea your work encompassed so much."

So *that* was what he was thinking. The discovery gave her a deep and quiet thrill of triumph.

It was as if a truce had been drawn between them and the past was forgotten completely. The quarrel, the long-standing enmity, the coldness—these had all been wiped out before the need, not only to draw together for Kitty's sake but also to understand what was being done for her. Dick's dark eyes, meeting Janet's above Kitty's head, revealed only a warm and admiring friendliness these days, while his voice, addressing her, held once again that caressing quality that could always make her heart turn over. Yet, standing there, poised and competent in her white uniform, her face calm, her wide hazel eyes steady and cool, Janet gave no indication of the turmoil he was stirring within her once more. Increasingly, however, she knew that some day they must talk. When or how this would come about she did not know. She only knew it was bound to happen.

It happened in November. There came a wild and windy day when snow sparkled and danced intermittently in the air whenever the sun burst through the banks of heavy, snow-filled clouds in the sky. Dick came alone that time, explaining that Molly had a cold and thought it best not to expose Kitty to it and Brent had had an appointment at his dentist's. It was, of course, a Saturday and Janet was on duty because—as usual—she had changed days with Rita or the third therapist employed there, so that she, Janet, might be present over the weekend when Dick appeared. Neither Molly nor Dick knew she did this but, today, Dick faced her suddenly with a question.

"Don't you Physical Therapists have a five-day week? How does it happen you're always here on Saturday and Sunday?"

"We—shift around," Janet answered, hoping Dick did not notice the color flooding slowly up into her face. If he did, he said nothing but turned instead to Kitty.

She lay flat on her back, her pony tails cut off short now, to make it easier to take care of her hair. Her two new teeth, large and white and strong, had filled up the gap in her mouth by this time and her smile was wide and radiant as she addressed her visitor, who stood above her with one hand held behind him.

"Look, Uncle Dick. I can move my arms a little now. The doctor lets me. So I can have a rack thing put up in front of me and I can read a book and turn the pages myself."

"That' s wonderful." He bent over her smilingly. "Somehow I must have known you could do that because look what I've brought you." And he produced a small, oblong package.

"A book!" she exclaimed. "It *is* a book, isn't it! Oh, let me open it myself. Is it the Fairy Tales?"

"That's just what it is," he answered.

Janet left them to chat together while she went to her

other patients. She was gone an hour and visiting time was nearly over when Dick sought her out, down by the desk, before taking his departure.

"Molly wanted me to ask what the last X-rays showed," he said.

She turned to him, her face alight. "Oh, Dick! They're very encouraging. The bones are knitting together nicely."

"But what does he say about her walking again?"

She shook her head. "Nothing definite. Although the doctor used the words 'very encouraging' himself. And the fact that she can move her toes by herself is encouraging, too."

He looked at her. "It takes a long time, doesn't it?" he asked.

"Yes, Dick, it does."

"All winter, I suppose."

"Oh, surely, all winter."

He was silent for a moment, then—"But you think by the end of it—"

She replied gently, "I hope, Dick. I just hope."

He nodded. "Of course. Well, that's what we're all doing." He paused. "I didn't see your car outside when I came in."

"No, I walked over this morning. It's so brisk and breezy out I love a day like this!"

"Are you through here soon?"

She glanced at her wrist watch. "In a half hour."

"I'll wait for you downstairs and drive you home." He hesitated, then added, with a small smile, "If I may?"

She nodded a consent, her heart thudding. "Thank you," she murmured.

She moved in a kind of trance through the next thirty minutes and when they were ended and she put on her warm cashmere coat, over her white uniform, she was still not thinking anything at all. Only one thing was clear. Dick was going to drive her home. What did that mean? Or didn't it mean anything?

It meant nothing, she decided, as she sat beside him in his little car listening to him talk of Molly, who had last week dismissed the practical nurse, Miss Pauly (whom Brent had engaged for her right after the accident) and was now getting along with the help of a high-school student who came to the house daily at four o'clock and remained through the dinner hour.

"So with Brent going to the office again and Molly's splints coming off in another week or so, things are almost back to normal there," he concluded.

"I'm glad."

He went on. "Molly says you've been going over to her in the evening, to give her massage and light therapy since Miss Pauly left."

"Yes, I've gone over about three evenings."

"That's awfully nice of you."

"I'm glad to do it. It'll make movement so much easier for her when she's allowed to use her arm again. It's conditioning, you know, keeping her muscles toned up. The same sort of thing I'm doing for Kitty, so that when she walks again—" She stopped.

He said quickly, "You said *when* and not *if*."

"Well, I'm believing that's the way it'll be, Dick. There have been other cases similar to hers in which there was complete recovery. I remember a boy—Pedro—in the Pres-

byterian Hospital who walked out by himself. He had to
wear a back brace, of course, as Kitty may, too."

He threw her a sudden smile and then there fell a silence. A moment later, he turned into her driveway and
stopped his car before the broad front steps, leaving his
engine running.

"Thank you for the lift," she said. Since he did not start
around the car to do it for her, as usual, she was reaching
for the door handle to get out, when, suddenly, he switched
off the motor.

"May I ask you a personal question?" He turned as he
spoke to look directly into her face, his eyes dark and demanding, the way she remembered them.

She answered, "Yes, what is it?"

"Molly has told me there's a rumor going around that
you and Scott Murray are engaged. I want to know if it's
true."

Her heart began thumping wildly, loudly, crazily.
Couldn't he hear it?

"No, it's not true," she told him. And then she saw the
dark demanding look vanish and in its stead warm twin
fires sprang to life in his eyes and he smiled and said, in
his most caressing voice, "In that case, may I come in with
you for awhile?"

She could only nod in reply, and they entered the house
together. Mrs. Moore, who was in the living room and
heard them, came forward, seemingly quite unsurprised.
She greeted Dick easily and not at all as if it had been
more than a year since he had been there. Then—"You'll
stay for dinner with us, won't you?" she asked, quite as a
matter of course. With equal naturalness, Dick replied,

"Thank you. I'd like to very much. May I telephone Molly I'm here?"

While he was telephoning, Janet escaped to her room, saying, "I'll go change out of this uniform." But once up there in that safe haven, she stood still before her mirror with both hands pressed to her hot cheeks as she whispered to herself, "What's going *on* here?"

It took her a long time to shower and dress because she had to get hold of herself. She must go down there and be as calm and casual as Dick was. . . .

When she finally appeared in her gold corduroy skirt and blouse, she presented (she hoped) as composed a manner as his. She even ignored the special pressure of her father's hand when he greeted her, because to acknowledge it with a return pressure was to admit its meaning. To admit that would be to shake everything with the threat of dissolution—her composure and the meaning of Dick's being here. If there was a meaning, she added.

It was an amazing evening. Was she dreaming it? Or was it real? Had time stopped? Or never been? And was this a continuation of the way things used to be? How could a gap be so easily closed? Yet it was—And without a word of explanation being said or even being necessary.

Yet words proved necessary eventually. As long as her parents were present, they weren't, but they excused themselves when they all had enjoyed their after-dinner coffee in the living room together—Mr. Moore to go out to a town meeting, Mrs. Moore to do some telephoning upstairs about the hospital. Then a silence fell and, in it, a constraint that seemed to put an impassable gulf between Janet and Dick.

It was he who bridged it. He had been standing as Janet's mother and father left the room. Now he came back to the davenport where she was sitting before the log fire and dropped down beside her. She felt him looking at her but she couldn't look at him.

"Janet."

"Yes?"

"I have a lot to say to you. First, I want to apologize—"

She turned her head then and met his eyes and gave a little gasp. "Oh, no! It's *I* who must—I've always wanted to after that awful night at the Country Club when I was so unbearably rude—"

Somehow, before she could finish, she was in his arms and he was stroking her hair and they were both talking at once.

"We never should have quarrelled. It was all my fault," she insisted.

"No, it was mine, because long before September— At the Inn, Jan, when you were telling me you wanted a career—I didn't know then that it was Physical Therapy you had in mind and I—"

She looked up at him and laughed a little. "How could you know? I didn't myself."

"—and I was sharp and intolerant—"

"But I was horrible to you, Dick. I said horrible things—"

"And you wouldn't come ski-ing with me to give me a chance to talk to you. Or have dinner with me when I tried to arrange a foursome—Or even talk to me on the phone. You kept calling Kay."

"Oh, I didn't *know,* Dick! I thought you wanted Kay. I didn't dream—"

"Silly stupid," he said softly.

So they talked, giving and forgiving, going over and over their mistakes and misunderstandings, thrashing them out until, finally, a silence fell. But this time it was a silence of contentment, of everything understood and all hurt wiped away and nothing left except a sweet peace. Out of it at last came words strangely familiar.

"Now let's make plans," he said. "Can't we be married this month?"

"This month!" Janet sat upright and stared at him out of wide, startled eyes. "Are you crazy?"

"No, I'm not crazy. I don't see why not." He smiled at her and then said, "I've already waited that year you wanted, you know."

"But—Dick!" She was aghast as she shook her head. "I'm under contract! I've signed up for a year of work here at the hospital! How could I possibly marry you and keep my contract? I couldn't commute from Connecticut daily! Besides, even if I could break my agreement with the hospital, there's Kitty." She shook her head again. "And Kitty is one patient I'm seeing through clear to the end of her hospitalization. I've promised myself that."

"Of course," he agreed, "I understand. You mustn't break your contract. And you must stay with Kitty. That, above all."

"Then what—how—" She was completely puzzled. "What are you thinking? You're not going to give up *your* job, are you?"

"No, but I can commute to Oakwood every weekend, the way I am now."

She stared at him incredulously. "You mean—really, you'd do that?"

"It's not the best arrangement, but it's better than waiting another year." He put his arm around her. "At least I think so. Don't you?"

"We'd just live here when you came, you mean."

"It seems sensible, doesn't it?" And she nodded in amazed agreement.

"It's a compromise," she said thoughtfully. "It's not what you really want. You are making a compromise, aren't you?"

"That's what life is—mostly—I've discovered."

"Perhaps." She looked at him a long moment. Then she said slowly, "There's one other thing. After my year here is up and I go to Connecticut with you—then what, Dick?"

"There are hospitals in Connecticut," he told her smilingly.

"You mean—"

He took both her hands and looked deep into her eyes.

"I mean that whatever you choose to do when we go there is up to you, Janet. It's entirely up to you. Your work is too worthwhile for me to ask you to give it up entirely. But how much time you'll put in on it is your decision to make." He paused. "I have a feeling, though, that you'll know how to compromise, too, and that you'll work it out fairly so you'll be successful both as a worker and as a wife."

ALICE ROSS COLVER

says of herself: "I was born into a comfortable way of life, where I was given the advantage of going to a very fine private school in Plainfield, New Jersey, and later to Wellesley College, from which I graduated with a B.A. degree. My four years there were dominated by my desire to become a writer. This ambition was put into effect soon after my marriage, when I wrote and had published the *Babs* series of books for girls. This was followed by the *Jeanne* series and later by novels. Since then, I have divided my time about equally between doing light fiction and stories for adolescent girls including the *Joan Foster* series, with a text book on writing, a biography and a couple of historical novels worked in between.

"The writing of all these books has not always been easy as I was the mother of three children, as well as an author, and my life with my husband required several moves to various parts of the country. I have lived in Arizona, California and Massachusetts, but have finally come full circle to my starting point in Tenafly, New Jersey. However, if these moves and my little family complicated life for me at times, they also enriched it, for I have used every place where I have lived as a background in my fiction and the adventures of my children have supplied me with much material for my juvenile stories. During the course of these years, I have had the excitement of witnessing the Hopi Snake Dance in its original setting, in Walpi, on the desert outside Flagstaff. I have lived happily in a small apartment in Redlands, California, and equally happily in a huge sprawling farmhouse in Stockbridge, Massachusetts. I have also had the fun of week-ending through two summers on a thirty-five-foot cabin cruiser.

"I suppose all this variety gave me an impetus to travel because, now that I am alone in life, I seize every opportunity to take a trip somewhere. I have been to the Caribbean, around the world once and to Europe twice—and am planning a third trip there. Aside from travel, I enjoy gardening, the theater, good books and good music, the study of languages in adult schools and old friendships."